Country World

also by Alison Uttley

ALISON UTTLEY

Country World
Memories of Childhood

—

Selected by Lucy Meredith

Illustrated by
C. F. Tunnicliffe R.A.

faber and faber
LONDON · BOSTON

First published in 1984
by Faber and Faber Limited
3 Queen Square London WC1
First published in this edition in 1986

Filmset by Wilmaset Birkenhead Merseyside
Printed in Great Britain by
Redwood Burn Ltd Trowbridge Wiltshire
All rights reserved

British Library Cataloguing in Publication Data

Uttley, Alison
Country world.
1. Country life—England—Derbyshire—
Juvenile literature   2. Derbyshire—Social life
and customs—Juvenile literature
I. Title
942.5'1081'0924   S522.G7
ISBN 0-571-13784-9

Contents

Alison Uttley was born and grew up on a Derbyshire farm, and her childhood provided inspiration and material for almost all her books. Of her three main works of autobiography, only *Ambush of Young Days* is in the first person; in *The Country Child* and *The Farm on the Hill* she writes of herself as Susan Garland, but Susan is clearly herself. This selection, drawn mainly though not entirely from these three books, takes her from her birth—a 'snow-baby'—in the bleak December of 1884 to her first day at the grammar school and the first break with her childhood and her country world.

L.M.

The Snow-baby

The north wind blew, the great solitary trees in the fields swayed and beat their branches together, cracking their thin twigs so that they were scattered on the ground. Sometimes a bough fell with a clatter that was lost in the roaring of the wind, a few swirling flakes of snow fell on the land, and the distant hills were misty.

Winter had come early and it was only the beginning of December. "Looks as if we are going to have a hard winter, for there's plenty of snow up yonder," remarked my father, nodding to the dark heavy sky. He went to the hall and tapped the barometer. "It's gone down low," said he.

"You'd better fetch the nurse early," said my mother, with a touch of anxiety in her voice. "Everything is ready for her. The bed in the little room is aired and the fire laid."

"Yes," agreed my father. "I'll take the cart and fetch her today. You'll feel more comfortable when she is here, my dear, and she can help in the house a bit and be company for you."

So after dinner he harnessed the mare in the spring cart, piled in a few rugs and drove down the hill and away to the distant village where the midwife lived. The snow was falling steadily, first in big flakes like feathers, and then in smaller flakes which swirled down so thickly the view over the fields to the surrounding hills was hidden. The mare walked slowly and carefully, shaking her head now and then to move the settling snow. She was sure-footed, and wise; she had been sharpened for the frost and ice and she

11

never slipped on the stones. She could be trusted to go without anyone holding the reins. She never swerved to one side as she passed through the gateways in the lane, but kept to the middle so that the wheels did not touch the gate-posts. My father wiped the snow from his face and stared out into the gathering darkness. He would have to light the candles before he got home, he told himself. The hills were invisible and the snow enclosed the cart and horse in a veil of delicate gauze.

The road was safely reached, and then the mare broke into a trot. The danger was over and she could run easily on the flat road by the river. She gave a snort and grunt as if to say she was happy to feel the firm ground under her hooves. My father softly whistled to her and chirruped, and she pricked back her ears and listened. She loved a whistle and she liked a song and the sound of a human voice. "Never mind the snow and the wind when my master is near me," said the mare to herself and she gave a little whinny.

The cart bowled along the road, skirting a wood, following the track of the river in the valley until a village was reached. The hamlet had only a few houses, and nobody was about. The roads were empty, and the mare turned up a long steep hill. She walked up the slope and my father moved forward on the seat to make it easier for her. The seat could be moved on small ratchets, to ease the weight on the shafts. At last they arrived at a hill village, perched on the upper slope of the climb, and my father stopped outside a wicket gate which led to a small grey cottage, in a row of cottages. Each had a long garden in front, separating it from the road. My father tied the reins to the brake, spoke to the mare, threw a rug on her back and went to the cottage.

The old nurse had been expecting him. She had a sixth sense, she knew things that would happen, and her bag was already packed with her clothes, her shawl and her bottles of herbal medicine and secret drugs. Soon she came out wearing her bonnet with a little frilled white cap under it, her cloak and her white apron.

She sat in the cart, huddled under a rug, warm and comfortable, and my father lighted the lamps, and drove away down the steep hill, along the valley and up the second big hill. All the way she talked, in a low country voice, and my father listened in silence and the mare also listened. They were in accord with this simple country woman who was so near to life and death.

What a welcome there was when she arrived in the house! The little maid, Patty, made the tea and took off her boots, and carried her bag upstairs. My mother kissed her and held her warm hands. My father stopped outside to unharness the mare and to pat her, and the servant lad, Willie, took her to the stable and rubbed her dry. He gave her some warm water and a feed of hay, and closed the door against the driving snow, which covered the yard two inches thick.

The elderly nurse quickly settled down, taking charge of the house, which she knew well. She helped Patty, and she helped my mother, she made gruel and she gave sips of herbal tea all round. She admired the baby basket with its muslin lining, and the little long-clothes prepared, with tiny stitches so small she had to put on her spectacles to see them. "Twenty stitches to an inch," she declared.

The weather got worse, the snow came down steadily all night and all the next day and every day. There seemed to be no end to it. Day after day it snowed, and soon the roads were impassable. No cart could go to the villages, for the edge of the road was level with deep drifts, and the gates were snowed under. No post or papers could come. The house was an island in the sea of whiteness. The stone walls between the fields were lost, they were covered in the drifts six or seven feet deep. A siege began, but each day my father and the lad, Willie, had to go out with spades to dig out a path from the farmhouse to the water troughs, to the stable and pig-cotes, and across the field to the cowhouses. The animals were secure and warm with their own breath, for snow is like a blanket and it keeps in the heat. The walls and roofs were thick and the houses built to face the tempests, and no winds could penetrate when doors and shutters were closed.

Milking had to be done twice a day, by the light of lanterns, and then the cattle were left to talk quietly to themselves, with food in the mangers and straw under-foot. Only the milkers suffered as they trudged slowly across the windswept field, wandering from the path, floundering in the snow in that exposed place, caught by the fierce gale which blew across the valley and up the hill, nearly smothering them with snow. When they got back to the house with their milk cans on the yokes, they were white and shivering, bitten by frosts, boots thick with snow. They rubbed their frozen hands with snow to heal them and dare not go near the fire. Their scarlet mittens did not protect the chilblained fingers. Their breath was frozen against the scarves they wore over their mouths, and their eyes streamed with water.

The baby would come soon, the nurse told everybody. There was no chance to get to the doctor through the drifts, but she could manage. There was food in the larder, baskets of eggs which could not go to the dealers, butter made from the new milk, cheeses, home-baked bread and a sack of flour ready for more bread, and a side of bacon. No one would starve. Onions, apples, carrots, potatoes were stored ready for winter, and the sugar jar was full to the brim with fifty pounds of brown sugar.

Fires were heaped with wood and coal, wood from the store in the barn, coal from the great open coal-place, where the ivy tods leaned over the walls. Everybody who entered the house stamped their feet to rid them of the snow, and the fires crackled and roared in the frosty air. Water was carried from the troughs each day after Willie and my father had broken the ice with axe-heads. Patty filled the shining cans with the sweet spring water, which looked black under the ice. Copper kettles were boiled and the large copper-pan was ready with hot water for any emergencies.

So I was born in this wild storm, with deep snow on the ground, and cattle shut in their houses, and horses in the stable. I was bathed in spring water heated over the fire, and I was held up to the window to open my eyes and to look out over the fields at the dazzling whiteness, and to look at the candles in their brass candlesticks, alight to welcome me.

After a few days I was taken downstairs, but first the nurse carried me in my long robe and shawl up the stairs to the attic. That was a tradition.

"A new-born child must always be taken up before it goes down, so it will go up in life and not down."

My first drink, after my mother's milk, was cinder tea. This was to allay the baby's thirst and it was made by dropping a red-hot cinder into a cup of water and allowing the child a sip of the luke-warm water. Sometimes a red-hot poker was used instead of a cinder, to take the chill off the icy water. It was a remedy old as the hills and perhaps it dates back to primitive man. Another drink was dill water for small pains and gripes, made from the seeds of the dill, and this simple cure is still in use.

I was wrapped in the long flannel nightdress over the thin lawn nightgown that babies wore, and laid in a drawer to sleep. There was no cradle, and the green wooden crib provided for me was too big for a baby. The old nurse took the deepest drawer from the polished mahogany chest of drawers, and lined it with blankets. She laid the drawer across two chairs and behold, a lovely cot for me.

The first flowers I saw were snowdrops from the orchard, picked to give my mother pleasure. The first vision of beauty came from the kissing-bunch which hung from a hook in the kitchen ceiling on Christmas Day, bright with glass balls and silver bells and little flags. The first stars I saw were the winter stars shining in the great dome of the sky. I was taken out in my mother's arms, wrapped closely in a shawl, to see the moon and stars, and to hear the lullaby sung to me:

> *"Twinkle, twinkle, little star,*
> *How I wonder what you are?*
> *Up above the world so high,*
> *Like a diamond in the sky."*

There was no perambulator for this child, for what was the use of an expensive baby-carriage where the land was so uneven the pram would run away if left? I slept in a clothes-basket, on the floor in winter, or in the garden in summer.

Icicles were nipped off the eaves where they hung like long thin men, and I ate one, nibbling the end, as if it were a lollipop, when I was one year old. I heard the curious squeak as an icicle was broken, and I laughed at it.

I was a snow-baby, a lucky baby, they said, born just before Christmas, in the great storm. Snow was part of my life, and it would always attract me and bring magic to me, magic of fairy-tale, and snow crystals and miracles of ice flowers on the windows.

Later, when I was three and four, I had my own tiny cup and saucer, and my own tiny teapot with "A present from Blackpool" written on the side. I poured out the mixture of tea and milk. The candles were lighted on the table and the shutters were closed. The musical box was wound up to play the tunes of Rossini, and my father played a hymn on his concertina. The winds blew and beat upon the house, but I felt safe with the thick walls and the rock beneath and my parents to take care of me. I played blind man's buff round the kitchen table, with the maid and the lad, or we sang carols.

I had only small presents, because Christmas was so near and my birthday gift was usually some article of clothing, a pair of woollen gloves, or warm knitted stockings, or a little red shawl which was twisted round my neck and tied under my arms to keep me warm. The real presents were the exciting magical happenings in field and wood and in the water troughs when the snow fell and the water froze. Snow was part of my life, an immortal possession for my birthday.

The Farm

The servant girl went to the trough with a bucket for fresh water, and I went with her. We stood waiting whilst somebody sprang through the green mossy stile, under the filbert-trees, and ran down the steep field to the pump. Homely sounds came floating from the meadows as we waited there—the whinny of a horse, the low moo of a cow, and the crow of a distant cock. In the dark yews the robin sang, the little bird which was never far from the back door, and the sweet smell of violets came from over the wall. There was a rustle of wind in the nut-trees, and a flecking play of sunlight made the shadows of the damson-trees, which hung over the deep troughs, dance on the water surface.

Then came the clank! clank! of the pump, and gulps as if some great animal struggled for breath, down in the earth. The icy flood sprang out of the leaden pipe with such force that it would have knocked the pail from the young woman's hand if she had held it near. Silver bubbles streamed up and all the water was in turbulent motion.

Together we counted aloud the fountains of water. "One, two, three, four, five, six." At the seventh, she held the bucket under the white gushing stream, until the water overflowed the edge and burst with violence into the trough.

"Cuckoo!" I called in a high treble, and I ran to the stile and looked far down to the moving figure at the pump wheel.

"Coo-oo-oo," I sang, and the servant girl added her voice to mine, pushing back her sunbonnet and struggling with the can. The sound rang down the valley, and the man turned his head. The pumping stopped but still the water flowed. Then a half-gurgle choked the pipe, and the fountain ceased. I dipped my little china mug into the bucket as the girl hauled it out on to the flags, and I drank the sweet water.

The memory comes back to me, and I taste the exquisite coldness of that pure water as I sipped it with tiny eager shivers of delight, long ago. The home of my childhood, eternal and green, appears before my inward eye, and I live again in the brightly coloured circle of hills where I was born. No matter where I am, I seek unconsciously for resemblances to that beloved spot. A draught of spring water, an uncut hedgerow, a broken wall, these bring back visions so real that I cannot tell in which life I am living, the present, or the crystal-clear past, when as a child I ran with arms outstretched to catch the wind down the well-known grassy hillsides.

In that green country with its cool deep valleys and fantastic rocks, the narrow paths wind over the hills, linking village to hamlet; they cross streams and wander through woods with ancient names, a thousand intersecting paths, which have been used by the countryman from Saxon times. From the highest parts one can trace the grass-covered roads, along which no cart travels. There are curling hedges which hold protecting arms round odd little fields, and dark lichened stone walls cutting and dividing the green, and everywhere there are woods, beech woods, a flaming fire in the back end of the year, soft as clouds in Spring, oak woods, rough and sturdy, plantations of dark fir and tender larch, and mixed woods of many colours and

sounds, sheltering fox and badger, woods full of enchantment.

A portion of that land I know so well that I can see the
contours of the hills, the patterns of the fields, the
irregularities of the diverse landscape as plainly as if they
were painted before me. I know every flower-filled ditch,
leafy hedge-bottom, and daisied bank, better than I know
the lines of my own hand, for during all my earliest years
my senses had no distractions from the daily scenes of
wood and field and hillside. They became part of me, like
the cold air I breathed, and I had no conception of other
lands beyond our own farm and its neighbourhood, the
countryside which filled the crumpled circle of England
displayed before my infant eyes.

My father, grandfather, and many generations before
them were born at the same farm, so that we felt we had
always been there, and spoke of the long dead as though
they lived. My great-uncle Timothy, who once lived at a
farm in the valley below, planted the walnut avenue which
led to his house a century before I was born. My
grandfather's father planted the tall fir-trees which were a
landmark for us from afar. Every tree or rock, highroad or
footpath seemed to carry a story. The land was tilled and
drained, new buildings were made, and each successive
son worked to make the poor land richer, giving his
strength to the earth, from which it came.

Agriculturally the soil on the hills is thin, for the rocks
are near the surface, and often they thrust their muzzles
through like black monsters. These stones were alive to
me, and I kept a wary eye upon them lest they should
move stealthily after me.

Even when I clambered upon them I felt as children do
when they are astride an elephant. I sensed the living

creature within, and although I had been in the triumphant position of the rider, I was glad to get some distance away and survey the beast, holding tightly to someone's hand. Up to the age of seven I was quite certain of the hidden life of stones, although I knew instinctively that I should be ridiculed if I mentioned the fact. Some rocks were friendly, they were shaped like seats or tables, they held ferns in their crevices, or they sheltered primroses and wild hyacinths. Others were sinister, and I walked backwards from them, or avoided them by circuitous paths, and pretences of looking· for something—shams which I feared the stones would recognize and remember.

A great stone across the valley was credited with the power of going down to the river to drink when it heard the cock crow. The laughing explanation that a stone can never hear a cock made no impression upon me, for I was convinced that all stones could hear. However, that particular stone was so far away, with many a field and the river between, that I didn't mind, and I stared across the lovely valley with only a mild interest.

The farm men said that stones grew, for every year they walked the fields with wiskets and picked up many basketfuls. This belief is current in many parts of rural England, I believe, and as sometimes I was allowed to take my little basket and walk up and down, gathering stones from the mowing grass, by the side of our old servant man, I heard many tales of stones appearing from nowhere, and stones growing larger each year.

The old house where my ancestors lived was partly rebuilt when my father was young, on the same foundations, with the same thick walls. I saw a water-colour painting of the older house when I was five, a stone gabled house with large red and white roses growing over it, and a rounded moss-covered wall surrounding it, similar to the house I knew, but the wall was now gone, and the grindlestone had been taken away from the lawn. This painting was stolen, soon after my father brought it out of his private oak chest to show to me, and we lamented its loss for years.

The centre of life for me as a child was the farm kitchen, where all was bustle and motion, where people passed and repassed, to save the longer journey round the house walls, on their way to farm buildings, or to water-troughs, where brilliant sunshine poured in at one open door, splashing the oak dresser and grandfather clock with light, where cool breezes fluttered at the second door, to the north, and milk-cans rattled with a gay tinkle of bells as they were lifted to the wall. From the window one saw the wide fields stretched out on the slope of the hills, a steep hillside of pasture and meadowland, with massed trees and little woods, going up to the sky. It was my world, our own farmland, and I watched the distant path to see my father and the men returning along it with cans of milk on their yokes, or going to the farm buildings with a flock of hens running after.

Inside, the room was gay with painted china, lovely patterned dishes, terra-cotta jugs with tiny faces on the handles, bright metals, warming-pan, horse-brasses, and polished oak furniture. There were smells of varying intensity, the scent of the wood-fire, and sticks in the kindling box, the sweet rank smell of rainwater, drugged with moss and ferns and decaying leaves of a past year, the strangely exciting smells of pepper and brine, of herbs and cowdrinks, of newly baked bread and strong tea, and also the animal smells which assailed my quivering nostrils, absorbing, breathing, taking in all around me—the smell of rabbits which were flung under the tallboy by my father as he hung up his gun, the smell of manure on boots, of horses and cattle, of stable and byre, all came surging into the farm kitchen, part of its life.

Every article in the cosy room had its own story, told to me many times. A deep oven built in the wall bearing a bright brass plaque with the words "Rumford Roaster, 1803", was the bread oven in my grandfather's childhood. The enormous preserving pan, half copper and half brass, large enough for a bath, was used in those days, and had been brimmed with plums and blackberries each summer ever since. No one knew the age of the brass saucepans which Patty cleaned with sand from the hillside. The heavy little fender was half a wheel from one of the first trains which had travelled on the line. The grandfather clock, with its shining brass face and round oak knobs, was almost human, for its tick changed in intensity, it spoke softly, or with insistent warning, hesitating, whispering, then hurriedly chattering to my listening ears.

The oak dresser was a most important piece of furniture, for servant men had eaten their meals at its beeswaxed surface for well over a hundred years, and the ends were scarred with their knives. The drawers were pitted with shot where a farm man jokingly aimed his gun at a servant girl at the beginning of the nineteenth century. Happily she had moved aside, and the shot spattered the front—a warning which was pointed out to every man, to unload before he entered the house.

In the drawers were neat piles of starched linen aprons, and in one drawer my mother kept the family Bible, and the books she was reading aloud. There I once found a book called *The Mystery of a Hansom Cab*. I began to read it, at the age of six, but I had scarcely finished the first page, when my mother saw me and took it away. It was a naughty frightening book, she said, and it disappeared from the house as mysteriously as it came.

On the dresser was a row of shining white metal canisters, polished bright as silver, like everything else in our house, filled with camomile, peppercorns, and spices of many kinds. They stood in descending heights on either side of the long oaken spoon-box, and I always thought they were relations, the smallest canister being myself.

At the end of the ledge on which they stood was an enormous dark-coloured pincushion, the Mother of Pincushions, heavy as if it were filled with lead, and very old. No one moved it; it squatted like an aged fat porcupine, bristling with giant needles and pins. Even the pins were unique, for many of them had once been darning-needles. When a needle's eye was broken, my mother put a little knob of sealing-wax on the end and made a scarlet-headed pin. Many a time I watched her do this, and the new pins lived charmed lives, for they never got lost. We took the greatest care of our pins, so that they were well-known, and I could have recognized some of the older inhabitants of the pincushion in a haystack of common little pins.

The names of the rooms were unaltered from olden days. Upper rooms were still called "chambers"—the apple-chamber, parlour-chamber, the lad's-chamber, the wench's-chamber, little chamber, and "the master's chamber". One of the parlours had become the dining-room, where we feasted on Sundays and holidays. At the end of the landing was a tiny room with a superb view over hill and valley. It was nobly panelled in rich old oak from the pews of the Parish Church, and many a delicate joke was made about the polished throne. The working of the crimson tassel and heavy woollen rope was a source of great wonder to me, and an annoyance to servants, for the water had to be pumped from the spring deep in the fields to the troughs, and then a second more homely little clanking pump, festooned with icicles and no use in winter, was used to bring the water aloft to a cistern. We were proud of this little room. Outside, along a mossy paved path, was the humble closet. It was overhung with crowns of fragrant red honeysuckle; musk grew at the door and flowered between the paving-stones. House-leek, green cushions of thick leaves and tall flowers, spread on its roof and formed a garden on the top of the screening wall. We had no bathroom, but large tin baths, white inside and elaborately grained outside, round, oval, square, deep and shallow, stood in the bedrooms, and in winter, by a roaring bedroom fire, it was the pleasantest way of bathing. Carrying water was so natural that nobody noticed it, and every day the kitchen boiler was filled from the troughs, the enormous "copper pan" on the stove was brimmed and lifted up by a man, water was carried upstairs, and taken to the back kitchen for churn-washing and other duties. The cattle and horses had their own troughs, in field and yard and grassy hollow, fed by springs which flowed underground in our land. The spring which fed the drinking-trough had never been known to go dry; legend said it was inexhaustible.

I knew every crack and cranny within the house, and the distinctive smell of each room, for every chamber had its odour according to its occupants and its furnishings, and I sniffed curiously as I pushed open doors and went into forbidden places. The parlour, with its casements opening on to grass-plat and flower-beds, was scented in summer with tea-roses and the warm paintwork of the shutters, but in winter there was a faint odour of mildew. The chintz covers on the chairs, the velvet couch, the pictures and ornaments all attracted me. There was the piano, too, which drew me like a magnet, and I pressed my fingers on the ivory keys whenever I crept into the room.

The dining-room, with its mahogany chairs and Chippendale sideboard, was solid and comfortable, a refuge from the noise of the kitchen, and there I went on secret exploration, climbing on a chair to look into the large cupboards which were built into the thickness of the wall, retreating under the table when footsteps drew near, peering through the fringe of the cloth at approaching feet. In the cupboards were old tea-services, gay with flowers, painted mugs, jugs and plates, with pictures of huntsmen, goddesses and nymphs. On the sideboard was the long musical box out of which came the most entrancing tripping melodies if I banged at the closed lid, and waked the little spindle.

I never had time to see all these treasures before somebody saw me through one of the three windows of the gable end, and dragged me ignominiously back to the watchful eyes of the kitchen.

Even there, where all the ornaments were displayed with an almost barbaric splendour, darkly gleaming guns hanging under the ceiling, bright Sheffield tankards and brass candlesticks on the mantelpiece, old china ranged on the dresser for everyone to see and admire, even there was temptation for me at three years old.

I waited until my mother went upstairs for her rest, and the servant girl, Patty, was changing her dress. Then I climbed on my own high chair, and opened the mahogany writing-desk on the dresser end. I expected to find something wonderful, like sealing wax, but all I could discover was stamps, which I promptly began to lick. At that moment, the door behind me opened softly, and my mother entered without my seeing.

"What are you doing there?" she asked in a severe voice. "Oh! How you *fightened* me!" I cried, accusingly, dropping the lid, caught in the act, and my mind raced for an excuse. Then I saw I had one, ready made, and I clambered down, satisfied that I was not in the wrong, for no one was allowed to "fighten" me.

In the hall was the Dark Passage, a space under the stairs, occupied by some furniture and a cupboard full of old china. The darkness was intense, and there my mother sat during bad thunderstorms which affected her. In that Dark Passage I was sent when I was naughty and there I stayed immobile, never venturing to sit down or peer into the brightness of the sunny hall, till somebody opened a door and called: "Alison! Are you good?" Then I answered gladly: "Yes, I'm kite good now," and I skipped out. I felt

better, changed by the purging darkness, where mice
scampered and rustled and where I expected to see
gleaming malignant eyes gaze at me out of the gloom. I felt
it was a just punishment for badness, and I never thought
of rebelling against the sentence, but walked meekly into
the black hole.

Except when I was exploring forbidden parts of the
house, I remained near the company, and followed the
servant or my mother into dairy or pantry or brewhouse,
to see what was happening in these lowly places with their
stone benches, and whitewashed walls, and smells of a
thousand strange things.

At night I trotted into the dairy, following Patty as she
went to get some cream. There stood the wide yellow
earthenware pancheons of milk in a row on the bench,
above my head, set for cream, for the butter-making. She
took a copper skimmer and swept the thick ivory-coloured
cream to fill the silver jug. The sweet smell of milk, the
harsh smell of the sanded benches, and the icy coldness of
the room filled me with awe and happiness so that I
hopped up and down on the flags. It was my home; the
dairy was a secret lovely place with little dripping sounds,
mysterious drops and flops, whilst outside the howling
wind shrieked round that North gable, slapping the trees
so that their branches crackled, sending cold draughts
through the gauze in a window-pane, swaling the candle's
narrow flame, so that it leapt like a dancing Irishman.
When the shutters were fastened the dairy was a room of
black and white, the milk and the whitewashed walls, and
the long black shadows which moved over floor and
ceiling as Patty peered for eggs and cheese, whilst I,
standing under the outstretched candle, was lost in a circle
of darkness. Then we returned to the kitchen, and I was

allowed to scrape the cream off the dipper with my finger, a velvety smooth delight.

In the pantry, round the corner, stood a great stone jar holding fifty pounds of Demerara sugar, into which I dipped my fingers when I was big enough to reach. Hams swung from the ceiling, and globes of lard like white cannon balls, whilst a side of bacon hung curing behind the door, startling me with its ugliness. On the bench was a large canister of Lipton's tea, with a picture of tea-plants and black girls. There were many packets of candles ranged along the shelves, tallow dips for the servants, suspended by their twisted wicks, and wax ones for ourselves, in the iron "Candle Bark", with tall fluted candles for the silver candlesticks, and stout little ones for the lamps of the pony-trap. Under the bench was an oak chest in which I kept my dolls and bricks and picture books. No toys were ever left lying about, and I had many a pang about this toy-box, which the mice seemed to think was their home. I drew out my dolls with quivers of fright, as a mouse leapt from under my fingers; I put them away with a hurried flight back to the room where all sat round in cheerful company.

I stood at the back door, hesitating on the step for a moment, blown by the wind. Then I ran to dip my mug in the trough for a drink of the cold water, or I skipped down the path to pigcote or garden, thrilling to the air, breathing it in with eager gasping breaths. Everyone who came to see us spoke of the "fresh air", and I knew what it meant. It was the icy sweet breath which filled my body as I stepped outside the door from the hot rooms, which ran its fingers through my hair and made it stand on end, which made my fingers tingle, and my heart beat with a queer excitement. It was a wind full of life, which I could taste and drink, as I ran across the yard to the farm buildings, and even "see" as it ruffled the long grass.

The oldest parts of the farm were very near, and the connecting link was the brewhouse, where all the farm beer was once brewed, and the old cottage, with a bedroom for farm men. A rose-tree grew over its walls, encircling the windows with red loose-petalled flowers, which had flourished there before my father's birth. The sliding shutters at the back of the cottage looked out on the steep drop of the hill, a romantic view which always excited me, for I was level with the tops of the great beech-trees in the wood below, and I looked into their green branches, where birds preened themselves, unconscious of my gaze.

The walls of the house itself were covered with a network of green branches, bearing flowers and fruit in their season. On one gable grew a pear-tree, whose pointed glossy leaves and clusters of blossom concealed many a bird's nest. The brown pears were gathered and carried away to ripen in safety in "the master's chamber". Next to it, bending its parallel branches round the corner, was a Victoria plum, a large tree with luscious red fruit which dropped with alluring thuds on the grass-plat below. Between these two, growing up the mullion, was a little red-flowered Japonica, a tree whose name gave me a peculiar satisfaction. I was strictly forbidden ever to pick a flower from this tree, and I gazed at it much as Eve must have looked at the tree in the Garden of Eden.

Honeysuckle hung in masses of bloom over the porch, but out of my reach. Next came my own tiny rose-tree, a daughter of the big tea-rose, climbing up the house front, like its mother. This great tree grew round the second gable, with flowers nodding at the bedroom windows, clambering to the roof. The scent filled the rooms, the delicate old-fashioned tea scent; the flowers were there from June to November, covering the wall with a profusion which made us grateful to Nature. We knew this tree in a personal kind of way, it was a descendant of still older rose-trees which had flourished there, in another century. We sent boxes of the creamy golden-hearted flowers away to friends and relations, and they seemed to carry with them the subtle essence of the farm itself.

Beyond this important tree came another honeysuckle, very old, whose heavy red crowns were mingled with the tea-roses on one side, and a web of thick ivy on the other.

The farmhouse stood like a castle on top of the hill, secure from the great gales of winter, sheltered by its line of stone barns and stables, cartsheds and cowhouses which clung, fortress-wise, along the hill's crest, built up from the rock itself. The greatest protection was given by an encircling wood of old beech trees, which covered the slopes below. This wood was the most beautiful of all the many woods around us—the larch plantation with its fairy tuffets of emerald green, the sturdy old oak wood which gave shelter to the main farm buildings across the fields, the fringe of woods which spread from east to north, bordering our land, and the great belt of woodland which swept across the southern horizon, dark woods which were full of colour and space when one entered them. They were too far away for my childhood explorations, they were the world's boundaries, where fierce wild beasts lived in caves, and I stared across at them, glad there was a tossing river between.

The vast trunks of the beeches in our guardian wood rose straight and smooth, like pillars of some lovely polished grey metal, from the moss-covered slopes, their branches forming a tent of delicate green through which the sunshine filtered on to the glowing surface below, making a pattern so tender, so intricate, as the branches gently moved in spring, that we involuntarily stopped to gaze at it, pulling up the horse for his wind, as we drove home under the walls of the wood. Tiny leaves of ivy trailed over the ground, the starry moss was heavy as a brilliant carpet. Nobody walked there, no flowers grew, few birds lived in its depths, but the airy beauty of it, caused by the mounting trees, spacious, majestic, climbing up the steepness to the high wall under the last crest, was like a noble symphony. From the back of the house we looked down the rocky incline to the tree-tops below us, from which a cock pheasant or a malign hawk flew to the other woods across the fields. It was a wood of enchantment, which I never entered, not only because I was too little to climb the high rough walls which protected it, but because I felt my own insignificance among those mighty trees, with never a tiny bush or flower to keep me company.

Under the shadow of the trees was a narrow croft, steeply sloping, like all our crofts, so that there was scarcely a foothold, except for the little green tracks made by the sheep. It was bounded by high black walls, but a secret little wicket-gate led to it. Here, one autumn, I discovered sweet chestnuts, to add to our store of filberts, hazels and walnuts, for there was a grove of the lovely trees on the wood boundary. There were drifts of brown beech-leaves in the broad ditch under the wall, and there we waded waist-deep, rejoicing in the sound of the rustling leaves. But it was a lonely field, a haunted little field, and I felt uneasy whenever I played there. Even the horses when turned into that croft stood by the wall at the top, craning over into the lane to get a glimpse of human company, whinnying when they saw anyone, and running alongside. Not a flower grew there, and the rabbits shunned it. It was the burial place for dead animals, and had been their cemetery for generations, and one felt their spirits move restlessly over its shadowed banks, seeking sunshine and the society of the farm. Yet, for a time, my brother and I played there, swinging on the long bough of a beech which dipped over from the wood below. We sat among the masses of leaves, and clustering beechnuts, and propelled ourselves from the steep slopes under our feet, rising and falling in rhythmic sweeps. Even this delight faded, and we left the little croft to its memories and departed to sunnier lands above.

In the open cart-shed, built into the side of the hill against the rock, were the heavy carts and the pony-trap. The light trap was behind a grille, for safety, but we were allowed to play in the empty carts. It was a game we loved. We each sat on a sloping seat, waved one of the whips that the servant boy had made of hazel switch and plaited string lash, and clicked, chirruped and called to an imaginary horse, whilst the carts rattled and banged along roads that led over the hills and far away.

Swallows built in the roof of the cart-shed, and mingled with the scent of earth and rocks was the pungent smell of birds' nests. The parent birds darted over our heads, unafraid of our noise. Sometimes the warm eggs were brought down for me to touch and wonder at, and then replaced by careful fingers. Swallows were sacred birds which must not be disturbed. They brought luck to a dwelling, and as they returned year after year to the same place, they were as much the children of the farm as we.

We were not allowed to play in some of the buildings, where mowing-machines and hay-choppers were a danger, but the barns were happy hiding-places. The warmth of the barns, even on a cold winter's day, the presence of trusses of hay, prickly gold, the smell of the neat pile of oilcake, and bags of meal, all made a heady intoxication which kept me in a state of excitement. There were queer things hanging on the walls, or hidden in dust on the window-sill. There was always something I had not seen before, some relic of long ago, forgotten until my spying eyes saw it. On the sill of the hay-barn across the fields I often found a bantam egg, put aside for my tea, or a double-yoked egg, a monstrosity like Humpty Dumpty, or a capful of mushrooms, a shot rabbit, or the pitiful corpse of a dead chick. On the wall hung an ancient horn, with the initials of four generations carved on it, my father's, grandfather's, and their forebears'.

The barn near the house had the most romantic junk, which I never had time to explore, for the door was shut and I was called away. There were old wooden cheese-presses with great stones weighing a couple of hundred-weights, and screw-presses, which nearly touched the rafters of the roof. There were enormous wooden corn-bins, too high for me to peep into, scythes and clubs and a broken spinning-wheel. On the stone bench our boots were cleaned, and I swung on the lower half of the door, watching Willie polish the boots, my father's large boots, so heavy I could scarcely lift them, my mother's elastic kid boots, or the slender buttoned boots just coming into fashion, and my own little lace-ups, stout and square. We talked of dogs and cats, rabbits and rats, always of animals he had known, and many a strange tale I heard, as the young lad brushed, until, when I leaned over, I could see a dusky queer smudge of a face in the surface of the bright shoe. Then "Whistle to me", I demanded, and I listened to bird imitations, to shrill calls, to dancing little tunes and sentimental ditties, in the smooth pure whistle of a boy.

Bonnets and Pinafores

In memory I see people towering above me, giants, just as they must have looked to me as a child, and their clothes have all the strangeness they had for me when I was under six. I am pressed against full striped skirts, with silver-buckled belts and pockets hidden in many folds at the back, or held to stout bosoms encased in hard whalebone stays. Bosoms alarmed me, especially the high-breasted kind. I preferred people to be flat, like my mother, without any protuberances, although, on the whole, I liked fat people better than thin ones. There was bead-trimming down many of these bosoms, which scratched my cheeks, or braid, in whorls and curls, twisting in fascinating spirals. The bodices had buttons of cut steel, or bright jet, or barrel-shaped braid buttons, but under this array was a row of hooks and eyes which fastened the lining, with its bones and stiffening.

Behind my mother's bedroom door and in her wardrobe were her dresses, of grey cashmere, of black silk, and of plum-coloured merino, with acorn-shaped buttons and silk buttons, with frills and ribbons and lace tuckers. There was a sweet scent about the clothes which I loved, and often I buried my face in the folds and sniffed for five minutes, breathing in the odour of some fragrant herb. I was sent to feel in the pocket for a lost handkerchief, or a purse, or keys, for pockets were so large they held a goodly number of things, but although I could feel the bulk of the pocket, I could not find my way in through the crowded pleats, and I struggled, standing on a chair to reach with my fingers impatiently trying to discover the hole. Sometimes I gave it up, and went downstairs without the object, only to be sent back for another attempt. The way a grown-up's pocket was concealed was always a mystery to me, for my own pocket was very conspicuous.

In summer my mother wore creamy holland dresses piped with white linen. Lizzie Wildgoose came from an upland cottage to stay for a week, to do the dress-making, and help with mending. My own little frocks were made from the same lengths of holland, with turned down collars and full sleeves. My brother and I wore holland garibaldis one summer, and we were very proud to hear they were named after a soldier. The name was a fine-sounding one, and I always said it with gusto, shouting "Garibaldi! Garibaldi!" when my clean starched blouse with its square collar came out of the linen drawer.

Over my dress I always wore a pinafore, of white starched linen, with lace frills round the neck and armholes. Pinafores and sashes were the most important articles of my apparel. The pinafore kept the dress clean, the sash adorned it. Every morning I put on a fresh pinafore, and I tried to keep it spotless, but at night it was soiled. On Sundays I had fine diaper pinafores with lace insertion, inherited from richer folk.

My dresses had rows of tucks, seven or eight, and as I grew they were taken out, so that the dress kept pace with me. It was a shameful thing to have a dress too short. The Sunday dress which I remember best, for I was photographed in it when I was five, was a honeycombed terra-cotta cashmere, with bishop sleeves, which crept higher and higher up my arms as I grew taller. It had so many tucks I wore it for years, its fullness kept in place by a wide red silk sash.

I wore fringed silk sashes on Sundays, over my loose dresses, and waistbands of starched holland on weekdays. There was an immense blue and white silk sash, half a yard broad, which was my best, a salmon silk for birthdays and tea-parties, and an Indian one for driving out. The sashes were put on with great care by my mother, fold after fold arranged round my waist in a pleated effect, and then a great bow was tied at my back, and I was set free from the long wait.

When I was three and a half I went to church wearing a red velvet bonnet and a caped coat. The bonnet was tall, with a stiff oval back, and a pleated crown, with a frill of red and white silk inside next to my cheeks. I remember the warmth of it over my ears and the shut-in feeling when the ribbons were tied under my chin. This bonnet was so much loved by my mother that she kept it for years. Whenever I opened a certain drawer I found my bonnet lying there, and I marvelled at its colour and richness. Other bonnets followed this, fawn and brown with beaver edgings.

Lastly, I had a grey cloak lined with scarlet and edged with fur, which was made by my mother and Lizzie. With it I wore a grey hood, also fur-bordered. It was a copy of Red Riding-hood's own head-dress, and was reversible, so that I was either in scarlet or grey. I was smothered in its thick folds, and I was aware that no one at church wore a hood like mine. We did not follow the fashions, we made our own styles, but my father was ashamed to be seen driving his pony and trap with a big girl of six in a bonnet beside him. His ridicule helped me to escape from the bondage of bonnets.

Sunbonnets, of course, were the summer wear for the fields and country journeys, and I had finely ruffled and pleated buff and pale pink bonnets, tied under my chin. For school I wore a round sailor hat with a blue ribbon dangling down the back.

When I had finished with bonnets I wore a Leghorn straw hat on Sundays in summer, and a "real beaver" with little pompoms on the side in winter. These hats served me for years, for "very best", and I had a real affection for them. When I was seven or thereabouts, I read a moral little story of a girl who grumbled at her clothes.

"Last year's hat!" she cried.

I couldn't understand this tale, for I loved last year's hat, with its dear familiar smell, its comfortable shape, adapted to my head, its bitter elastic. The elastic particularly enamoured me, and the narrow band under each hat had its own characteristics. I knew where it was smooth, where it was knobby with frayed edges, and the knot in the middle, where it had been tightened, was a friend. Elastic under the chin was a solace to a lonely child, like the touch of a beloved hand on one's face. It was food on a long walk when pangs of hunger assailed me, and I nibbled and sucked the elastic under my everyday hat as I walked the miles to school. I held it with one finger when I was frightened, to give myself confidence, and, when I was happy and carefree, I swung my hat by it, or let the shady straw hang down my back, held to my neck by the loop.

Unfortunately my mother didn't like my bitten tangled elastics, and every few weeks she insisted on putting in a fresh one. After the first few hours of strangeness, I made overtures to it, and once more I had a companion.

Every Sunday, when I took off my Leghorn hat, I was told to stuff the pink bows with tissue paper to keep them upright, before I put it away in its box. My beaver hat was wrapped in a large handkerchief before it was placed in the hat drawer. It was necessary to take great care of one's Sunday clothes.

My clothes were plain and few, from the white chemise which I wore next my skin, to the top layer of frock and pinafore, and everything was home-made except the Liberty bodice on which my stockings were fastened. Buttoned to the bodice were white drawers with Torchon lace around the edges. I was proud of my drawers, garments which must never be seen or the disgrace was terrible, but I remember comparing the lace edges with those of another little girl at school, lifting my skirt and showing my finery with a desperate boldness as I tried to impress her. Under my frock was a white petticoat in summer and a hand-crocheted scarlet one in winter.

I needed all the warmth I could get, for I went to school in all weathers, walking through snowstorms and torrents of rain, thunder and lightning. Soon my clothes were wet through, I had no mackintosh, nor did I ever see one among the children. My little umbrella was often swept from my grasp, and turned inside out, an occurrence which filled me with chagrin, for boys laughed as I struggled with the broken ribs and torn cover. I could not manage an umbrella, and I preferred to go without. I arrived at school or at home, wet to the skin, but happy and warm with my struggle against wind and rain.

My capes and cloaks were my comfort, and I wrapped them tightly around me, and bent my head, on which was perched a tam-o'-shanter or a round tweed hat to match my cloak. Then the wind could blow and the rain pour. I went to the schoolmaster's house and took off my wet dress, and sat by the fire draped in somebody's dressing-gown whilst my clothes dried, thankful to miss lessons for a time. At the mature age of six I returned home from a visit to a relation wearing a "bustle" under my dress. It was a black cushion, heart-shaped, hard as iron, tied round my waist with two long tapes. The bustle made the back project in the absurd town fashion, which had never penetrated to our own simple countryside. When my mother saw me wearing this atrocity she quickly untied it and threw it in the fire, to my satisfaction, for I was afraid to remove it myself.

The servant girls wore lavender or blue-sprigged cotton bonnets when they carried water from the troughs or clothes to the orchard, or when they helped with milking in times of short labour. White caps were a later innovation. These girls loved to go milking, and when my father went to the big cattle-market at our country town, or to the various agricultural shows, the maid took his place in the cowhouse, for milking had to be done at the same time, and the milk sent to the station whatever happened.

The print bonnets hung behind one of the doors in the kitchen, and when I was three or four a smock frock belonging to old Josiah hung there too. He was an old man

who lived with us for many years, and he brought old ways with him, such as my father had known in his youth. He wore a smock frock of coarse white linen, handwoven by his wife, with elaborate work across the front. When he went milking he put this on, to keep his clothes clean, and very delightful I thought it was, although I was surprised to see an old man in a pinafore.

My father, too, wore a smock when he was a young man, he told us. A smock was a garment to be proud of, for clever fingers made it, and the linen was strong and evenly woven. Smock-making for her three sons was one of the occupations of my grandmother, and she made them from start to finish. It took months to make a good smock, I was told. She had a spinning-wheel which stood in the corner of the kitchen, between the fire and the window, and there she spun, and laid down the law, governing with a firm hand her big family of which my father was the youngest. My father's clothes were made by the tailor, chosen from the very best cloth, cut and fitted with as much care as if they were the Squire's. The trousers were made in the style of the 1860s, a fashion he would not have changed. He always chose finely striped greys and with the suits he wore spotted blue satin cravats which the tailor made for him. The material never wore out, and many years later one saw these clothes on old men who had once worked for us. He had many pockets in the large loosely fitting coat, and the waistcoat, too, had odd extra pockets for secret things. These pockets were a source of wonder to me, for he put his hand in one, and then in another, bringing out strange things, especially after he had driven to the town. Out would come sausages, sweets, cartridges, a toy trumpet, a doll, a musical box, a bottle of liniment, a box of pills, a new pair of spectacles, a bag of rosy pears, more and more things, till one stared as if he were a conjuror, and my mother protested that he would spoil the shape of his coat.

"What are pockets for if you can't fill them?" he would ask, and I wished I had more than my solitary pocket, which hung at that time, like Lucy Locket's, dangling from my waistband, a gathered bag.

My father wore enormous square top hats, quite unlike anyone's else's, one for the village and a best one for the market town. He was most particular about his clothes and hats, and before he went out we ran round him with brushes and whisks, my mother smoothing and brushing his hat, the servant brushing his topcoat, I whisking his trousers, and the servant boy polishing his boots. In the Dark Passage hung a beaver top hat and a Balaclava cap, but these we kept for Dumb Crambo.

I was the chief putter-on and puller-off of boots, and I carried them to the barn to be cleaned by the boy, and then tugged and pulled to draw them on my father's feet. I was reprimanded for my carelessness in this work, for I never unloosed enough laces, and the struggle was dour, as my father pushed and I pulled. When he returned from his journey, or from the farmwork, I sat at his feet to remove the boots. I tugged, and fell over backwards every time, rolling over the hearthstone, as the great boot was suddenly loosened and his foot slipped out.

There was keen rivalry between my brother and myself over these boots, and we each took one foot, as my father sat back at his ease. Then we got the warmed slippers from the fireside and dragged them on. This operation always took place in the kitchen, for nobody ever went into the sitting-rooms or bedrooms in boots.

It was an important piece of work, which an autocratic

man appreciated, and when we were older this duty was taken on by the servant boys.

A truly ancient man, whom everyone called "Uncle All-sopp" although as far as I know he was no relation, used to come to see us when I was very young. He arrived unexpectedly and dramatically, riding over the hills on his pony. One of us, looking out of the windows, would suddenly exclaim: "There's somebody riding down the Top Pasture. Is it Uncle Allsopp? It looks like his smock frock." Then I ran outside and waited for him, and the rest of the house prepared a meal. He sat in the kitchen, with his big face wreathed in white whiskers, and I listened to his talk which I couldn't understand, for he used old words and a broad dialect. He wore a smock, snowy-white, and very beautifully worked, admired by all of us. I sat on his knee, holding his enormous stick, and smelling the harsh fragrance. Even in those days he seemed to have come out of another century. He was independent, both in means and appearance, and he refused to change his ways or bow to modern fashions. People whom he met stared at his odd figure, but he passed the time of day, and rode calmly on. He was very old, he must have been born before Trafalgar, but I was too little to ask any questions of those times. I stared at him, and fingered his smock shyly, and watched his toothless jaws. His face was ruddy and smooth, his eye like a bird's quick-spying everything, his movements, though slow, had no uncertainty. He could give and take a joke, for I remember the laughter and gaiety of the venerable old man, whom nothing could disturb, until Death came and they walked serenely off together to the green fields of heaven.

An old lady, too, visited us when I was four. Her hair was worn in a chignon, hanging at the nape of her neck. She wore a black satin apron in the afternoon, embroidered around with rosebuds and leaves in coloured silks. It was very beautiful to me, and I loved to sit on her warm lap, and feel the softness of the satin, and the bumpy touch of the embroidery against my hands. I thought the flowers would open, the closed buds would swell to big flowers. When the apron was folded up on the baby-basket on the dresser, I used to stare up at it, high above my head, and struggle to climb up and touch it.

Colours interested me very much, and embroideries fascinated me, for I thought they were real creations, like God's. There was a great tiger-lily which my mother had embroidered soon after her marriage, a beautiful piece of work. I sat near this for many minutes in silent rapture, moving little fingers across the silky stamens, and the long curling petals of the flower. Usually it was hidden behind a muslin cover, and I begged for a sight of this lily whenever I went in the parlour. Another cushion, whose splendours were too delicate to be exposed to the air, gave me a feeling which I recall very vividly. I throbbed with excitement and joy when the cover was removed from this precious cushion, and the work could be seen. It was another piece of my mother's handwork, a coarse linen completely covered with long stripes of coloured silks, each line embroidered in a different stitch like a sampler. There were lavenders and turquoise, azures, soft emeralds and jades, every colour that existed in the embroidery world, all pale and faintly old-fashioned, with no strong note, so that it seemed like an air from the musical box which stood on the sideboard nearby. Narrow ribbons of velvet were stitched with invisible stitches, tiny gold beads adorned it like gems. Nothing of the background was to be seen, and the whole tapestry of colour gave me an extraordinary happiness, as if I gazed at a web from fairyland. If I could have

47

carried it off and hidden it in a hole in a tree, I would have done so. I had an aching desire to possess it, to absorb it into my being. Even with the muslin over it I could trace the silks and ribbons with my fingers and imagine the splendour within.

In the wine drawer of the Chippendale sideboard was a pillowcase filled with embroidery silks, and my mother had this by her side when she worked at her mantel-borders and cushions on winter evenings. This bag gave me some of the joy of the two cushions, for the same colours were there. There was a shade of purple which made my fingers tingle, and a rose colour which was like the heart of a flower. I dipped into the bag one day when I was alone in the room, and took some skeins of the colours I adored. I also chose some of the shreds of silk and velvet which my mother kept for her patch-work quilting. I was eight, and could sew very well, so I determined to make a beautiful thing all by myself secretly, for I knew I couldn't have the lovely silks. I started off to the seat under the pear-tree at the end of the garden, and there, alone with the bullfinches and blackbirds, I tried to make a patch-work cushion.

I sewed a few pieces together, but they cockled, having no paper stiffenings. Then, eager to use my silks, I feather-stitched round the edges. The colours were discordant, the pattern was wrong, I couldn't blend the silks, I knew I was spoiling my work, and making only a cobble. The needle was sticky and refused to go through the velvet, and my conscience made me feel miserable, as I thought of the theft.

In church the next Sunday a sermon was preached which threw me into a fever of repentance. All the prayers seemed directed against my sin, but I never thought of confessing. I fetched my little bundle from the play-box and threw it in the fire. As the flames curled round the lavender and rose silks I felt a great relief. Sin and patchwork had both disappeared in the fire, and I felt free once more, purged of my wicked desires.

Dark Wood

The dark wood was green and gold, green where the oak trees stood crowded together with misshapen twisted trunks, red-gold where the great smooth beeches lifted their branching arms to the sky. In between jostled silver birches—olive-tinted fountains which never reached the light—black spruces with little pale candles on each tip, and nut trees smothered to the neck in dense bracken.

The bracken was a forest in itself, a curving verdant flood of branches, transparent as water by the path, but thick, heavy, secret, a foot or two away, where high ferny crests waved above the softly moving ferns, just as the beech tops flaunted above the rest of the wood. The rabbits which crept quietly in and out reared on their hind legs to see who was going by. They pricked their ears and stood erect, and then dropped silently on soft paws and disappeared into the close ranks of brown stems when they saw the child.

She walked along the rough path, casting fearful glances to right and left. She never ran, even in moments of greatest terror, when things seemed very near, for then They would know she was afraid and close round her. Gossamer stretched across the way from nut bush to bracken frond, and clung to her cold cheeks. Split acorns and beech mast lay thick on the ground, green and brown patterns in the upside-down red leaves which made a carpet. Heavy rains had swept the soil to the lower levels of the path, and laid bare the rock in many places. On a

sandy patch she saw her own footprint, a little square toe
and a horse-shoe where the iron heel had sunk. That was
in the morning when all was fresh and fair. It cheered her
to see the homely mark, and she stayed a moment to look
at it, and replace her foot in it, as Robinson Crusoe might
have done. A squirrel, rippling along a leafy bough,
peered at her, and then, finding her so still, ran down the
tree trunk and along the ground.

Her step was strangely silent, and a close observer
would have seen that she walked only on the soil between
the stones of the footpath, stones of the earth itself, which
had worn their way through the thin layer of grass. Her
eyes and ears were as alert as those of a small wild animal
as she slid through the shades in the depths of the wood.
A mis-step made her iron heel catch a stone, and the sharp
ring alarmed a blackbird dipping among the beech leaves,
but it frightened the child still more. She gasped and held
her breath, listening with all her senses, her heart beating
in her throat. A little breeze rustled, lost among the trees,
seeking its parent wind, fluttering the leaves as it tried to
escape. Then it flew out through the tree tops and was
gone, and she was alone again.

Every day she had this ordeal, a walk of a mile or more
through the dense old wood, along the deserted footpath.
A hundred years ago, before the highway was made, it
was a well-worn road between the villages of Raddle and
distant Mellow. Now it only went to Windystone Hall, and
everyone walked or drove along the turnpike by the river,
deep in the valley, two hundred feet below.

No-one ever knew Susan's fears, she never even
formulated them to herself, except as "things". But
whether they were giants which she half expected to see
straddle out of the dark distance, or dwarfs, hidden behind

the trees, or bears and Indians in the undergrowth, or even the trees themselves marching down upon her, she was not certain. They must never be mentioned, and, above all, They must never know she was afraid.

It was no use for her to tell herself there were no giants, or that bears had disappeared in England centuries ago, or that trees could not walk. She knew that quite well, but the terror remained, a subconscious fear which quickly rose to consciousness when she pressed back the catch of the gate at the entrance to the wood, and closed it soundlessly, as she entered the deep listening wood on her way home from school in the dusky evenings.

In the middle of Dark Wood the climbing path rose up a steep incline, too steep for Susan to hurry, with black shadows on either side. Then it skirted a field, a small, queer, haunted-looking field of ragwort and bracken, long given to the wild wood, which pressed in on every side. A high rudely-made wall surrounded it, through the chinks of which she was sure that eyes were watching. To pass this field was the culmination of agony, for she had to walk close to the wall in the semi-darkness of overhanging trees, and nothing could save her if a long arm and skinny hand shot out.

At the top of the field, which sloped up the wood, was a tumble-down building, which was the authentic House that Jack built, with rats and malt complete, but long ago it had been deserted and now Fear lived there. Once she saw a battered man creeping through the bracken towards the ruin, but he never saw the little shadow with a school bag on her back slip past the mossy gate of the field.

Beyond the ragwort field was a fair open stretch of wood, with cow-wheat and delicate fumitory growing by the path. The trees were not so close together, and a glimpse of the blue sky came through in summer, or a star in the winter.

The child's heart ceased its heavy pounding and she took in deep breaths in readiness for the next ordeal, an immense rugged oak tree which waited at the cross-road, where her path cut across two others. One way led downhill to a cottage in the fields below the wood, a path no-one used. The other went up the steep sides of the wood past great boulders which lay among the trees like primitive beasts crouching in the dark, until it faded away to nothing in the bracken.

But something was behind the oak tree, hidden, lurking, and the leaves all watched her approach. She threw back her head and stared boldly at it, but her feet were winged for flight as she slipped softly along. Once, two years ago, when she was seven, a pair of eyes had looked at her from behind the tree, and once a dead white cow had lain there, swollen and stiff, brought to be buried in the wood.

A nut tree stood in her path, low, human, but it was friendly, and always she touched its branches with fluttering trembling fingers, receiving solace from the warm twigs, as she passed on to meet the oak. She held her head sideways, pretending to look up at the scrap of sky, but her eyes were peeping behind, like a scared rabbit's, and the tree seemed to turn its branches and look after her, whilst the thing, whatever it was, skipped round the trunk to the other side. She never turned to look behind her, but trusted to her sense of hearing, which had become very acute with the strain imposed upon it. She whispered a little prayer, a cry to God for help, as she left the tree behind.

Then she walked down the tunnel of beech trees, for the oaks were left behind and the character of the wood had changed. The trees thinned and the beeches rose clear of undergrowth with massive smooth grey trunks from the carpet of golden leaves. Susan breathed naturally again, and walked rapidly forward, heeding neither rock nor tree, her eager eyes fixed on the light ahead. The evening sunshine streamed through the end of the path, a circle of radiance, where a stile and broken gate ended the wood.

Nothing could get through these, and she sang in a tiny quavering voice, for she still trembled a little, just to show the things she didn't care, as she entered the fields beyond. From the gate it was not far to her home on the hill-top, and sometimes she could see her mother, standing on a bank, silhouetted against the sky, anxiously looking for the little speck of a girl, and waving a teacloth up and down like a white flag when she saw her come out of the dark doorway of the wood.

Little Susan Garland walked four miles every morning to the village school at Dangle. It was the only school, and to it went the minister's children, the struggling doctor's, the girls from the saw-mill, boys from the water-mill, children from remote farms and little manor houses, where they couldn't afford a governess, children from tiny cottages and small shops, and rough little people from a long row of stone dwellings, whose parents lived how they could.

She ran gaily through the Dark Wood without a glance at the oak tree, or the ragwort field, or the dark patches of mystery, black even in the morning sunlight. Everything was asleep and nothing could harm her. The path was downhill, and she felt free and careless as a squirrel or one of the brown birds flitting across the fields, very different from the wary, watchful child who tried to slip unseen through the wood at night.

Fairy tales always brought her companions, and she walked homewards down the long road from Dangle to

Raddle with four or five girls hanging round her in a bunch, arms encircling waists, heads close together, as she told them of the Princess and the Golden Bird, or the Palace of Ice. The girls lived at Raddle, a hamlet of pretty thatched cottages, a post office and a general shop, a mile and a half from the school and half a mile from the Dark Wood, so when they were at home Susan had two miles further to go alone.

When she saw the village approaching and the time for parting, and the lonely walk through the wood getting near, she brought her story to a climax and kept it there with the bribe:

"Walk part way through the wood with me, and I'll tell you the rest."

On hot summer afternoons the children came with her over the bridge, past Lane End Farm, and up the steep fields which led to the wood. Young stirks and companies of hens scattered before their laughter and shouts as Susan told her story. She lured them on into the wood, but soon the silence and gloom depressed them and they hesitated. "We must go home now, it is tea-time, I promised I wouldn't be late," they excused themselves uneasily, and back they ran as fast as their legs would go. In the autumn and winter they never put a foot in the wood, and travellers walked round by the road which was a mile longer when they went to Mellow.

As Susan climbed the last hill, on top of which her home was perched so that it looked like a watch-tower against the sky, her mind became calm and her thoughts leapt forward to the house. She walked by the high wall of the orchard, which was covered with berried ivy and clustered with blackberry bushes, but no evil eye stared through its chinks, no face leered from the apple trees. She stopped for breath and looked over the valley laid out like a tapestry of green fields and black walls, dark firs with flat boughs still against the sky, the Dark Wood with its rounded tree-tops curving on the hill-side out of sight, and the little green path disappearing into its solitude. She opened the big white gate, and shut it with a clang behind her, as a challenge, sending the sound down, down, across the fields to the wood to tell "Them" she was safe.

The yard dog, Roger, barked violently and then changed his frantic rush to a welcoming wag of his whole body as he saw the queer little familiar person skip round the corner, waving her hat and snapping her fingers at him. He stood wistfully looking after her as she walked up the garden through the little wicket gate to the side door. Then he returned to his kennel and lay there, fastened with a heavy chain to the rock at the door of his square stone house, listening, hoping, waiting.

Susan flung open the door of the farmhouse and threw down her bag on the oak dresser.

"Well, have you been a good girl to-day, Susan?" asked Mrs. Garland, as she kissed the warm lips Susan held up to her.

"Yes, Mother, quite good," said Susan, hesitating.

"Have you had the cane?" continued her mother.

"Yes, for talking, but it didn't hurt," replied Susan calmly, and she hung her hat and coat behind the door, and washed her hands in the brass bowl standing on the sink.

Mrs. Garland set a plate of hot meat and vegetables for her by the bright fire, and as she ate it she told the story of the day's adventures, omitting any reference to her fears in the wood. Even when the girls at school said, "Aren't you afraid to go through that wood alone, Susan Garland?" she denied it, for it would never do to say her fears aloud, or somehow They would know.

After her meal she played outside in the dusk, running races with herself, skipping up and down the cobbled farmyard, tossing a ball in the air to hit the sycamore tree, singing and talking to Roger, who ran up and down, nearly wild to get loose. Then she met the farm men walking slowly home with the cans of milk, steadying them with both hands as they swayed on the yokes across their shoulders. She collected the eggs from the window ledge in the barn where Becky had left them and carried them to the dairy in a large flat basket. The men put the milk-cans in the stone troughs at the back door to cool whilst they harnessed the horse.

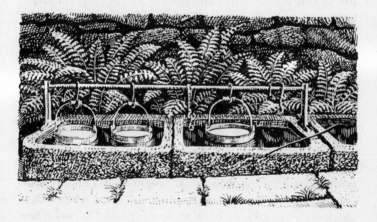

"Susan, Susan, come and stir the milk," called Tom Garland, and Susan ran out and seized a hazel wand which lay, clean and bright, across the troughs. She dipped it in the frothy foamy pails and swirled the milk round and round, sending little splashes of cream over into the water, watching them fall like funnels of opal deep down till they became one with the water. The stars came out and twinkled in the great clean-water trough, and she dipped her wand in to break them into fragments.

"Come on, that's enough. You're spilling the milk and messing the drinking water. Get away, you're no use," and her father pushed her aside to take the milk to be measured.

Dan took the lantern with him to light his way back from the station, and the cart rattled away down the hill. Tom Garland and Joshua went into the kitchen and Susan ran in too. Margaret lit the lamp and set it in the middle of thee table, and they drew up their chairs for tea, but Susan curled up like a kitten in the corner of the settle under the row of shining measures and graters, sieves and colanders. She put her fingers in her ears and lost herself in *Swiss Family Robinson*.

Her library consisted of four books, *Robinson Crusoe*, *Swiss Family Robinson*, *Nicholas Nickleby*, and Hans Andersen. She read them in turns, over and over again. This was the sixth time of reading, but the stories were ever new.

The tea things were cleared away, the milk cart returned and Dan sat down to his meal at the end of the dresser by the hall door. Becky washed up the milk cans and sieves, rattling them on the stone sink, laughing and talking, but Susan read on through all the clatter, even when black shadows fell across her book as people passed between her and the lamp.

At eight o'clock Mrs. Garland gave her a little pink mug full of creamy milk and a slice of bread and dripping. She fetched a candle from the old Candle Bark in the pantry, and went upstairs to her bed in the attic.

Dark Wood

As she left the bright hot kitchen and walked up the stairs she thought of the fox on the landing, the stuffed fox, shot when Susan was a baby by Tom Garland, who found it coming from a hen house. It stood between two windows and its glass eyes followed Susan wherever she went. Never did she lose the feeling that the fox's soul was hidden in his furry body. She could stroke him and touch his eyes with her fingers, and carry him in her arms, but she dare not turn her back on him. So she walked sideways past him, up the stairs to her own bedroom under the roof. The attic stair creaked and she loved the comforting sound, which talked to her. She knew it would cry out if the fox came up in the night.

So she shut the door of the whitewashed room and quickly undressed, whilst her long shadow dipped and mowed and cowered on the crooked ceiling.

It ran over the big mahogany chest of drawers, full of clothes belonging to past generations of Garlands, and hesitated, lingering on the little crib under the eaves where Susan used to sleep with it. It leapt off the carved oak chest, when she put the candlestick to rest there, whilst she washed in the tiny blue and white flowery bowl sunk in the green washstand behind the door. In that oak chest the bride of "Mistletoe Bough" had hidden—Old Joshua recited it every Christmas—and her skeleton was found twenty years afterwards by her sorrowing husband. Nothing could shake Susan's belief this was the veritable chest, and she kept a Bible on the top, just in case the bride might lift the lid and pop out.

The window was a tall narrow slit with iron bars, for the attic hung over a cliff with a sheer drop at the back. A great elm tree, growing in the shallow soil which covered the rock, lifted up its boughs and threw in handfuls of yellowing leaves when the window was open. Its murmur always filled the room with whispers, for even on the hottest day its branches waved to and fro, catching every breath of air on that high slope to which it clung, and the little twigs trembled and tapped at the glass.

Down at the bottom of the rock, under the encircling beech wood, rabbits played and stoats crept stealthily from the walls. Often Susan lay with misery in her heart, listening to the piercing screams of the small wild things caught by their enemies, and she sprang out of bed to scare them away. Hawks hovered level with the window, so that she could see their fierce bright eyes before they dropped on a tiny mouse far below. She would creep upstairs when she ought to be peeling potatoes or practising her music, to stare out across the fields and little woods to the tall beech trees which waved their plumy crests against the sky.

But at night, when she had said her prayers and crept into the immense wooden bed with its four round balls like heads at the corners, she could see nothing but the boughs of trees and stars shining through. She lay thinking of the *Swiss Family Robinson*, imagining further adventures in which she was the resourceful heroine, forgetful of the terrors of the day, heedless of the morrow, and so she slept.

December

December was a wonderful month. Jack Frost painted ferns and tropical trees with starry skies over the windows, hidden behind the shutters to surprise Becky when she came down in the morning.

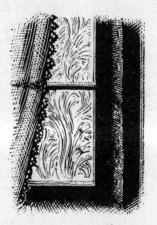

"Look at the trees and stars he's made with his fingers," she called to Susan, who ran from the kitchen to the parlour, and into the south parlour and dairy to see the sights. It really was kind of him to take all that trouble, and she saw him, a tall thin man with pointed face and ears, running round the outside of the house, dipping his long fingers in a pointed bag to paint on the glass those delicate pictures.

"Look at the feathers the Old Woman is dropping from

the sky," cried Becky, as she opened the door and looked out on a world of snow.

"They are not feathers, it's snow," explained Susan impatiently. Really Becky didn't know everything.

"And what is snow but feathers," returned Becky triumphantly. "It's the Old Woman plucking a goose."

Susan accepted it and gazed up to see the Old Woman, wide and spreading across the sky, with a goose as big as the world across her knees.

"Hark to the poor souls moaning," Becky cried when the wind called sadly and piped through the cracks of the doors. "That's the poor dead souls, crying there," and she shivered whilst Susan stared out with grieved eyes, trying to pierce the air and see the shadowy forms wringing their hands and weeping for their lost firesides and warm blankets as they floated over the icy woods.

But at Christmas the wind ceased to moan. Snow lay thick on the fields and the woods cast blue shadows across it. The fir trees were like sparkling, gem-laden Christmas trees, the only ones Susan had ever seen. The orchard, with the lacy old boughs outlined with snow, was a grove of fairy trees. The woods were enchanted, exquisite, the trees were holy, and anything harmful had shrunken to a thin wisp and had retreated into the depths.

The fields lay with their unevennesses gone and paths obliterated, smooth white slopes criss-crossed by black lines running up to the woods. More than ever the farm seemed under a spell, like a toy in the forest, with little wooden animals and men; a brown horse led by a stiff little red-scarfed man to a yellow stable door; round, white, woolly sheep clustering round a blue trough of orange mangolds; red cows drinking from a square, white trough, and returning to a painted cow-house.

Footprints were everywhere on the snow, rabbits and foxes, blackbirds, pheasants and partridges, trails of small paws, the mark of a brush, and the long feet of the cock pheasant and the tip-mark of his tail.

A jay flew out of the wood like a blue flashing diamond and came to the grass-plot for bread. A robin entered the house and hopped under the table while Susan sat very still and her father sprinkled crumbs on the floor.

Rats crouched outside the window, peeping out of the walls with gleaming eyes, seizing the birds' crumbs and scraps, and slowly lolloping back again.

Red squirrels ran along the walls to the back door, close to the window to eat the crumbs on the bench where the milk cans froze. Every wild animal felt that a truce had come with the snow, and they visited the house where there was food in plenty, and sat with paws uplifted and noses twitching.

For the granaries were full, it had been a prosperous year, and there was food for everyone. Not like the year before when there was so little hay that Tom had to buy a stack in February. Three large haystacks as big as houses stood in the stack-yard, thatched evenly and straight by Job Fletcher, who was the best thatcher for many a mile. Great mounds showed where the roots were buried. The brick-lined pit was filled with grains and in the barns were stores of corn.

The old brew-house was full of logs of wood, piled high against the walls, cut from trees which the wind had blown down. The coal-house with its strong ivied walls, part of the old fortress, had been stored with coal brought many a mile in the blaze of summer; twenty tons lay under the snow.

On the kitchen walls hung the sides of bacon and from

hooks in the ceiling dangled great hams and shoulders. Bunches of onions were twisted in the pantry and barn, and an empty cow-house was stored with potatoes for immediate use.

The floor of the apple chamber was covered with apples, rosy apples, little yellow ones, like cowslip balls, wizenedy apples with withered, wrinkled cheeks, fat, well-fed, smooth-faced apples, and immense green cookers, pointed like a house, which would burst in the oven and pour out a thick cream of the very essence of apples.

Even the cheese chamber had its cheeses this year, for there had been too much milk for the milkman, and the cheese presses had been put into use again. Some of them were Christmas cheese, with layers of sage running through the middles like green ribbons.

Stone jars like those in which the forty thieves hid stood on the pantry floor, filled with white lard, and balls of fat tied up in bladders hung from the hooks. Along the broad shelves round the walls were pots of jam, blackberry and apple, from the woods and orchard, Victoria plum from the trees on house and barn, black currant from the garden, and red currant jelly, damson cheese from the half-wild ancient trees which grew everywhere, leaning over walls, dropping their blue fruit on paths and walls, in pigsty and orchard, in field and water trough, so that Susan thought they were wild as hips and haws.

Pickles and spices filled old brown pots decorated with crosses and flowers, like the pitchers and crocks of Will Shakespeare's time.

In the little dark wine chamber under the stairs were bottles of elderberry wine, purple, thick, and sweet, and golden cowslip wine, and hot ginger, some of them many years old, waiting for the winter festivities.

There were dishes piled with mince pies on the shelves of the larder, and a row of plum puddings with their white calico caps, and strings of sausages, and round pats of butter, with swans and cows and wheat-ears printed upon them.

Everyone who called at the farm had to eat and drink at Christmastide.

A few days before Christmas Tom Garland and Dan took a bill-hook and knife and went into the woods to cut branches of scarlet-berried holly. They tied them together with ropes and dragged them down over the fields, to the barn. Tom cut a bough of mistletoe from the ancient hollow hawthorn which leaned over the wall by the orchard, and thick clumps of dark-berried ivy from the walls.

Indoors Mrs. Garland and Susan and Becky polished and rubbed and cleaned the furniture and brasses, so that everything glowed and glittered. They decorated every room, from the kitchen where every lustre jug had its sprig in its mouth, every brass candlestick had its chaplet, every copper saucepan and preserving-pan had its wreath of shining berries and leaves, through the hall, which was a bower of green, to the two parlours which were festooned and hung with holly and boughs of fir, and ivy berries dipped in red raddle, left over from sheep marking.

Holly decked every picture and ornament. Sprays hung over the bacon and twisted round the hams and herb bunches. The clock carried a crown on his head, and every dish-cover had a little sprig. Susan kept an eye on the lonely forgotten humble things, the jelly moulds and colanders and nutmeg-graters, and made them happy with glossy leaves. Everything seemed to speak, to ask for its morsel of greenery, and she tried to leave out nothing.

On Christmas Eve fires blazed in the kitchen and parlour and even in the bedrooms. Becky ran from room to room with the red-hot salamander which she stuck between the bars to make a blaze, and Margaret took the copper warming-pan filled with glowing cinders from the kitchen fire and rubbed it between the sheets of all the beds. Susan had come down to her cosy tiny room with thick curtains at the window, and a fire in the big fireplace. Flames roared up the chimneys as Dan carried in the logs and Becky piled them on the blaze. The wind came back and tried to get in, howling at the key-holes, but all the shutters were cottered and the doors shut. The horses and mares stood in the stables, warm and happy, with nodding heads. The cows slept in the cow-houses, the sheep in the open sheds. Only Roger stood at the door of his kennel, staring up at the sky, howling to the dog in the moon, and then he, too, turned and lay down in his straw.

In the middle of the kitchen ceiling there hung the kissing-bunch, the best and brightest pieces of holly made in the shape of a large ball which dangled from the hook. Silver and gilt drops, crimson bells, blue glass trumpets, bright oranges and red polished apples, peeped and glittered through the glossy leaves. Little flags of all nations, but chiefly Turkish for some unknown reason, stuck out like quills on a hedgehog. The lamp hung near, and every little berry, every leaf, every pretty ball and apple had a tiny yellow flame reflected in its heart.

Twisted candles hung down, yellow, red, and blue, unlighted but gay, and on either side was a string of paper lanterns.

Margaret climbed on a stool and nailed on the wall the Christmas texts, "God bless our Home", "God is Love", "Peace be on this House", "A Happy Christmas and a Bright New Year".

Scarlet-breasted robins, holly, mistletoe and gay flowers decorated them, and the letters were red and blue on a black ground. Never had Susan seen such lovely pictures, she thought, as she strained up and counted the number of letters in each text to see which was the luckiest one.

Joshua sat by the fire, warming his old wrinkled hands, and stooping forward to stir the mugs of mulled ale which warmed on the hob. The annual Christmas game was about to begin, but he was too old to join in it, and he watched with laughing eyes, and cracked a joke with anyone who would listen.

Margaret fetched a mask from the hall, a pink face with small slits for eyes through which no-one could see. Then Becky put it on Dan's stout red face and took him to the end of the room, with his back to the others. Susan bobbed up and down with excitement and a tiny queer feeling that it wasn't Dan but somebody else, a stranger who had slipped in with the wind, or a ghost that had come out of the cob-webbed interior of the clock to join in the fun. She never quite liked it, but she would not have missed the excitement for anything.

Dan stood with his head nearly touching the low ceiling. His hair brushed against bunches of thyme and sage, and he scratched his face against the kissing-bunch, to Joshua's immense satisfaction and glee.

Becky and Susan and Margaret stood with their backs to the fire, and Tom lay back on the settle to see fair play.

"Jack, Jack, your supper's ready," they called in chorus, chuckling and laughing to each other.

"Where's the spoon?" asked Dan, holding out his hands.

"Look all round the room," they cried gleefully.

"Can't see it," exclaimed Dan as he twisted his neck round to the shuttered windows, up to the kissing-bunch, and down to the floor.

"Look on top of All Saints' Church," they sang.

Dan turned his mask up to the ceiling.

"Lump of lead," he solemnly replied.

"Then catch them all by the hair of the head!" they shrieked, running and shouting with laughter.

Dan chased after them, tumbling over stools, catching the clock, hitting the row of coloured lanterns, pricking his neck, and walking into doors, cupboards and dressers.

Susan ran, half afraid, but wholly happy, except when the pink mask came too near and the sightless eyes turned towards her, when she couldn't help giving a scream. Joshua warded him away from the flames, and Tom kept him from upsetting the brass and copper vessels which gleamed like fires under the ceiling.

Susan was caught by her hair and she became Jack. Now she put on the strange-smelling mask, and with it she became another person, bold, bad, fearless.

So it went on, the old country game, whilst Margaret kept stopping to peep in the oven at the mince pies and roast potatoes.

Next came "Turn the Trencher", but Dan couldn't stop to play, for he had to be off a-guisering. He blacked his face with burnt cork and whitened his eyebrows. He borrowed Becky's black straw hat and wrapped her shawl round his shoulders. Then off he went to join a party of farm lads who were visiting the scattered farms.

He had not long been gone, and Tom was spinning the trencher between finger and thumb in the middle of the floor, when the dog barked as if someone were coming.

"Whist, whist," cried old Joshua.

"Hark," cried Tom, stopping the whirling board, "there's something doing."

They heard muffled steps coming down the path to the door.

"It's the guisers coming here," cried Tom, and they all stood up expectantly with eager faces and excited whispers.

> Here we come a-wassailing
> Among the leaves so green,
> Here we come a-wandering,
> So fair to be seen.
>
> We are not daily beggars
> That beg from door to door,
> But we are neighbours' children,
> Whom you have seen before.
>
> Call up the butler of this house,
> Put on his golden ring,
> Let him bring us up a glass of beer,
> And better we shall sing.

Here they pushed open the door and half entered.

> *God bless the master of this house,*
> *And bless the mistress, too,*
> *And all the little children*
> *That round the table go.*
>
> *And all your kin and kinsfolk,*
> *That dwell both far and near,*
> *I wish you a Merry Christmas,*
> *And a happy New Year.*

"Come in, come in," shouted Tom, with his broad face wreathed in smiles. Half a dozen young men and a woman stamped their feet and entered, bringing clots of snow and gusts of the sweet icy air. Their faces were masked and they disguised their voices, speaking in gruff tones or high falsettos, which caused much gay laughter.

They stood in a row in front of the dresser, and asked riddles of one another.

"How many sticks go to the building of a crow's nest?"

"None, for they are all carried."

"When is a man thinner than a lath?"

"When he's a-shaving."

"Who was the first whistler, and what tune did he whistle?"

"The wind, and he whistled 'Over the hills and far away'."

"What is that which a coach cannot move without, and yet it's no use to it?"

"A nose."

Tom and Joshua knew the answers and kept mum, but Becky and Susan were busy guessing, Margaret too.

Then Tom said, "Now I'll give you one.

> *"In a garden there strayed*
> *A beautiful maid, as fair as the flowers of the morn;*
> *The first hour of her life she was made a wife,*
> *And she died before she was born."*

The guisers made wild guesses and Tom sat back, smiling and gleeful.

"No, you're wrong, it's Eve," he said at last in a tone of triumph.

"And here's another," he continued:

> *"There is a thing was three weeks old,*
> *When Adam was no more;*
> *This thing it was but four weeks old,*
> *When Adam was four score."*

The guisers gave it up, and Susan, who had heard it many a time, could scarcely keep the word within her mouth, but Tom frowned and nudged her to be quiet.

"'Tis the moon," he cried, and they all nodded their masks.

"Here's one," said Joshua:

> *"I've seen you where you never were,*
> *And where you ne'er will be;*
> *And yet within that very place,*
> *You shall be seen by me."*

When they couldn't guess it and had murmured, "You've seen me where I never was" many times, he told them, "In a looking-glass."

"Eh, Mester Taberner," cried one. "You've never seed me in a looking-glass," and they all guffawed.

"And I know that voice," returned Joshua, "'tis Jim Hodges from Over Wood way."

"You're right, Mester Taberner," said Jim, as he removed his mask and disclosed his red cheeks.

So the guessing went on, until all the mummers were unmasked, Dick Jolly, Tom Snow, Bob Bird, Sam Roper, and Miriam Webster.

They drew up chairs to the fire and Susan got plates and big china mugs, and the two-handled posset cups. Margaret piled the mince pies, as big as saucers, on a fluted dish and handed them round.

"Help yourselves, help yourselves, 'Christmas comes but once a year, and when it comes it brings good cheer,'" said Tom, and he poured out the spiced hot ale for the men, and the women ate posset with nutmeg and sugar.

When the guisers had eaten and drunk, old Joshua rose to his feet to give them all his Christmas piece, "The Mistletoe Bough".

Susan listened to the poem she knew so well, repeating it after him under her breath. She knew that poor bride would get in the oak chest, there was no stopping her, but she felt thankful that when she herself went to bed it would be in the Little Chamber, and not alongside the fatal chest in the attic. But she loved to hear Joshua tell the story in his old cracked voice, which quavered when he was excited.

The guisers stamped in applause, and clapped their hands. They put on their masks, saying, "He's got a rare memory," and stood up to sing a last song.

Then, calling good wishes, greetings, blessings, tags of wit, they left the farm, and stumbled with lanterns and sticks across the fields to Oak Meadow.

"That Miriam should not go a-guisering with those men," said Becky indignantly, when the door was shut, and they returned to the fire. "She should think shame of herself."

She flounced off to her own chair, by the dresser, for she and Dan never sat in the family circle.

"'Tis an old custom, that," observed Tom, as he leaned back against the comfortable cusions of the settle, "but when my father was young and his father before him, they did a play, a mumming play, with no words."

Then he told stories of his childhood, which Susan enjoyed more than anything, of Windystone in far-away days, when the dead-and-gone lived there. He told how they brewed their own beer in the brew-house, and made their tallow-dips. His grandmother sat in the chimney corner with a spinning-wheel, and made the very same cloth they had on the table. He told of the horse thief who stole the mare out of the orchard, and how he would have been hanged if they had caught him. He told of the mesmerists who gave entertainments in Raddle and Dangle, hypnotizing the people with passes of their hands so that they did whatever they were told. He told of the ghost his father met by the gate in the meadow, which never answered but brought death to the house. Strange, grim stories, which Susan would never forget.

"Tell the funny tale of the man who sold his wife," she implored when Tom paused.

"There was a man, lived at Leadington, he went by the name of Abraham Maze. He couldn't get on with his wife."

"Don't tell that tale before Susan," interrupted Margaret indignantly.

"Why, what's the matter with it? There's no harm in it! It's a warning to cacklers," and Tom looked round the company as if he accused them all.

"Well, as I was saying, he couldn't get on with his wife. She had such a tongue, it went nineteen to the dozen, never still a moment, clatter, clatter, clatter all day and night too.

73

They led a regular cat-and-dog life, and she drove him to drink, although he was a steady fellow.

"Well, he was talking about her one night at the Pig and Two Faces, that's the name of the inn at Leadington, it's a farmhouse too. There's a sign of a pig with half its face laughing, as it might be, and half scowling."

"Yes, I knows it," said Joshua, "I've been there many a time to lend a mare for their muck-carting. They were short of a horse."

"Well," continued Tom patiently, "he told the folk about his wife, and everybody was right sorry for him, although they couldn't help laughing at him for being so henpecked. Then a stranger asks, 'Will you sell her?'

"So he says, 'Right willing I will, if anyone wants to buy such truck.'"

"Then it was very rude and wicked of him," cried Margaret, "to talk about his wife like that."

"Will you be quiet!" Tom was exasperated, "How can I tell a tale if you will keep interrupting? 'How much do you want, Master?' asked the man.

"'Sixpence,' shouts Maze, banging his fist on the table. 'You can have her for sixpence, that's all she's worth.'

"'Done,' shouts the other fellow, 'sixpence I'll give.'

"So he paid the sixpence right there, and went home with Maze. She went away with the other man that very night. I forget his name, he was a Frenchy that bought her."

"And what happened then?" asked Susan, wondering in her heart if anyone would sell her when she was grown up.

"She lived with him for a few weeks, and then she ran away and went back to her first husband. And the funny thing was, he was glad to have her back again, to mend his stockings and cook."

"Matrimony's a terrible queer thing," said Joshua, and he shook his shoulders and felt in his pocket for his snuff-box, to clear his head.

"Matrimony and sorrow begins," said Susan dreamily, "matrimony and sorrow begins." She did not know what the words meant, but she lifted up her young face to gaze into Joshua's deeply furrowed old cheeks, his thick white hair, and his tender mouth. He was thinking of his dead wife and the trouble he had had.

"Do you know what that is, Joshua?" she asked, putting her hand on his knee to wake him from his dream.

"I ought to know, Susan," he replied.

"It's bread and butter, Joshua, with a piece of cake between. The bread and butter is sorrow, you know, and the cake is matrimony. I have it for tea when I'm good," she explained.

"I used always to call it 'Matrimony and Solla beggins'," she laughed.

"We've had both," said Margaret, stroking her husband's hand, "but we've not had the sorrow many people have had. We've a lot to be thankful for."

The clock rattled its chain and took a deep loud breath as it drew itself up ready to strike. Then slowly, loudly, brooking no interfering conversation, it chimed nine o'clock, the last stroke singing on as if it were loath to leave the warm comfort of the dark cobwebbed interior, to venture out into the brightness of the kitchen and away through the keyhole and chimney, into the great lonely world beyond.

"In three hours it will be Christmas Day," continued Margaret. "The shepherds are out on the hillside, minding the sheep, and the star is shining in the sky. Get me the Bible, Susan, and I will read the chapter."

Susan took the old brown leather Bible from the dresser where it lay ready for use by the spoon box, and laid it on the table in front of her mother, who searched among the little texts which lay within for the place.

Joshua and Tom sat up straight to listen, Susan drew her low chair to the fire, and Becky sat down in her correct place as servant at the bottom of the table.

The wind thumped at the door, so that the latch rattled, and cried sadly as it tried to get in to listen to the tale. The flames licked round the bars and held their breath as the old words dropped peacefully in the room.

"And it came to pass in those days that there went out a decree from Caesar Augustus that all the world should be taxed."

Joseph and Mary went to Bethlehem on a dark night to pay their tax, and there was no room for them at the inn. How cold it was, snow everywhere, and perhaps wolves prowling round, thought Susan, as the wind howled under the kitchen door. They walked up and down, up and down, till they found a stable, and she thought of them walking across the fields stumbling against rocks and trees, in deep snow, to the stable in the cobbled yard underneath the weathercock.

There Jesus was born and put in the manger. The ox and the ass stood watching and Joseph had a lantern to look at the little Baby Boy. But afar in a field some shepherds were minding their sheep and they saw a star. Susan knew which one it was, it shone through the fir tree across the lawn.

The star moved, just as the moon moved when it brought her home through the wood in winter, and the shepherds left their sheep and followed it.

The sheep were not lonely that night because it was like

day with that big bright star in the sky, and a host of angels floated in the air, singing, "Glory to God in the Highest, and on earth peace, goodwill toward men." The sheep stopped eating to look up at the angels, but they were not afraid.

The shepherds followed the star till it came above the stable, and there it stopped, in the branches of the elm tree. The stable door was open, and the little horseshoe in the upper door shone in the starlight, and the brighter light from within came streaming out to meet them. It was warm inside, with hay and the animals' breath, so the Baby and Mary sat cosily in the manger. Mary's feet were tucked up so that she could get in with the Holy Child, and bits of hay and straw were sticking to her blue dress.

Susan could scarcely keep the tears from her eyes, she was so excited over the story she knew so well. If only she had been there too, a little girl with those shepherds, she would have seen the Wise Men ride up on their camels, through the gate into the yard. They carried gold and frankincense and myrrh, yellow gold as big as a lump of coal, and myrrh like leaves, smelling sweeter than lavender or mignonette, and frankincense, something, she didn't know what, something in a blue and gold box with red stones on it.

Then Mrs. Garland put a little embroidered cross in the Bible and closed its pages reverently. She took off her spectacles and laid them on the table, and they all knelt down to pray.

They prayed for the Queen and Country, for the three doves, Peace, Wisdom, and Understanding, and they thanked God for all the blessings of this life.

But Susan's head began to nod, and she rested it on the hard chair. When the others arose, she still knelt there, fast asleep.

So her mother roused her, and she said "Good night, God bless you," for anyone might disappear in the night, and they went upstairs together to the Little Chamber, where a fire burned in the grate, and shadows jumped up and down the ceiling, fire-shadows the best of all.

She hung up her stocking at the foot of the bed and fell asleep. But soon singing roused her, and she sat up, bewildered. Yes, it was the carol-singers.

Margaret came running upstairs and wrapped her in a blanket. She took her across the landing to her own room, and pulled up the linen blind.

Outside under the stars she could see the group of men and women with lanterns throwing beams across the paths and on to the stable door. One man stood apart beating time, another played a fiddle, and another had a flute. The rest sang in four parts the Christmas hymns, "While shepherds watched", "Come all ye faithful", and "Hark, the herald angels sing".

There was the star, Susan could see it twinkling and bright in the dark boughs with their white frosted layers, and there was the stable. She watched the faces half lit by the lanterns, top-coats pulled up to their necks. The music of the violin came thin and squeaky, like a singing icicle, blue and cold, but magic, and the flute was warm like the voices.

They stopped and waited a moment. Tom's deep voice came from the darkness. They trooped, chattering and puffing out their cheeks, and clapping their arms round their bodies, to the front door. They were going into the parlour for elderberry wine and their collection money. A bright light flickered across the snow as the door was flung wide open. Then a bang, and Susan went back to bed.

December

Christmas Eve was nearly over, but to-morrow was Christmas Day, the best day in all the year. She shut her eyes and fell asleep.

Village Names

In our two villages, both distant from our home, yet ever in our conversation, were many people with surnames which were mysterious and intriguing to the young mind, for the name carried an attribute which we attached to the owner. We never would have agreed with Shakespeare:

> *What's in a name? That which we call a rose*
> *By any other name would smell as sweet.*

If a man were named Broom he must in some way resemble that familiar and useful object, but Mr. Broom, aristocratic and rich, never wielded a broom himself for he had gardeners to do it for him. This was a puzzle, but the world was a strange and unpredictable place.

Mrs. Fox, who lived at a neighbouring farm, a long, low house with Seven-Sister roses growing on the front and a wild stream in the pretty garden, was in league with the foxes in the woods which surrounded her home and ours. It took years for me to be unafraid of her sweet, old-fashioned face and her gentle Quaker manners and I had to be cajoled and comforted when she came to see us. "Fox ate chickens," I murmured.

So the names of the villagers were deeply significant, and I still remember them with the added embellishments of my own imagination. There were Buntings who went to school with me, and "Bye Baby Bunting, Father's gone a-hunting" they were. I was at ease with all of them from the shoemaker in his little shop in one village, wearing his black apron and bringing out his kid boots for me to try on, to the little boy Bunting with Eton collar and bow tie and corduroy jacket and red cheeks who was in my class. Peach was another boy but I looked on him with disfavour. The fruit was unknown although I had seen peach stones and the servant boy had carved one into a basket for me, but clumsy and untidy Peach was not like a peach stone at all. Wildgoose was an enchanting name, romantic in its implications, and Wildgoose was the title of the fishmonger and seller of game in the little town by the river where we drove once a week. I sat in the trap watching him, in his straw hat and striped blue apron, and as he weighed the fish or stroked a pheasant's feathers I regarded him with curious eyes, waiting for him to rise up with hidden wings and fly across the river and over the limestone cliffs, away and away to join his friends and relations in the wood. I never spoke to him, I only gazed intently while the adults shopped.

Rose was a farmer and happy he must have been with such a name and such a garden as he possessed. Mr. Savage was rather alarming through his name and I kept my distance. Mr. Yeoman also was a farmer and one of his children went to school with me. I knew that we were yeomen, too, farmers of long lineage. Mr. Wheatcroft was a church-warden and at Harvest Festival when he read the lessons he made me think of a field of golden wheat in spite of his immaculate morning suit.

Clay was heavy and dull and so were the children called Stone. Slater lived on a hill farm among the rocks and the heather, and the name and the people suited the rocky country. Hill and Dale were well-known country people whose names seemed to fit into the county of hills and dales, and Brook was a nice watery name. Smith was a blacksmith, naturally, and Oak and Ash were names we knew, with Lamb, Hogg and Kidd. Pride was another fishmonger in a distant town where we went sometimes but I felt uncomfortable as I watched from my shelter in the trap. He belonged to the "Seven Deadly Sins" and I was often warned by Puritanical people against pride.

Wood and Allwood were good names with plenty of trees and timber about them. The little daughter of the latter sang like a blackbird for she lived among woods and trees. Dockerill and Docksey were horsy names allied to Dobbin and my parents trusted them to be faithful and true. Our sewing mistress was named Farmer, which gave me confidence in her. Middleditch, Hedges and Nightingale were local country names, with familiar associations. Snowball and Frost were schoolchildren with unsatisfactory names, for one expected to be cold in their proximity. Marsh, too, was a displeasing name for me and I never felt happy with a child whose name was so wet and boggy. Lee and Lane, Green, White and Brown were all comfortable names for us to recognize and associate with the owners.

Lawyer Limb always carried the title of his profession, and Gentleman Radford, wearing spats and carrying a little cane, followed by a small Yorkshire terrier, was a personal friend who always raised his bowler hat to a little girl going to her music lesson. There were no Diamonds but a Gold was the corndealer and again it was an appropriate name as he dealt in the golden wheat and hay.

No great or noble names were in the annals and the only strange one was Ollerenshaw. We were simple people cut off by the hills and when our history master said that the son of the village blacksmith in a small market town might be descended from the great family of Howard of Elizabethan days, we were much impressed, and young brave Howard went up in our estimation as a possible future warrior and commander.

We should never have agreed that a name was of no account at all. A name was all-important to our way of thinking. A brave bold name was a great help in time of trouble; who could be brave with the surname of Meek or Coward?

Country Nights

Like a traveller to an inn the darkness came, and everything was made ready. The lamps had already been trimmed on the stone bench in the kitchen, but they were not lighted till darkness arrived. It would be a waste to light them too soon. There they stood, the parlour lamp with its heavy bronze base, and its white globe round as the full moon, sprinkled with frosty stars; the kitchen lamp of brass, with its reflecting shade like a wide-brimmed hat and the little hand lamps for dairy and hall, as well as the stable lantern with its horn panes. The milking lanterns had already gone to the cowhouses and soon their bright nodding beams would come over the fields and across the yard. The great fire illuminated the room and Susan and her mother stooped close to read and sew by its flickering, dancing flame. Every scrap of light was garnered, and they worked in the dusk, with quick glances at the window to see if the milking lanterns were alight, and then at the shadows which crept out of the corners of the room to share their company. Over the low ceiling ran those shadows; a tousled beggarman came from the stout string bag, a tall hobgoblin from Becky's sunbonnet and thick skirt behind the door. The fire gave bright eyes to the warming-pan, and the tins and cans winked maliciously. The sanded hearth was yellow as the fire that beat down upon it, and Margaret kept her slippers away from its smooth cleanliness. Susan sat in the chimney corner, and behind her the wall was festooned with a row of shining utensils, each one to be used, each one a household friend and companion to her.

The blowbellies were there, ready to puff the fire, the wooden hands to smack the butter, the great iron poker to stir up the flames, and the cudgel to take in haste to a wild cow or escaping bull. On the hooks hung skewers and hatchets, a pair of tryes and a copper skimmer, an egg-beater, and a long steel and sieves. Each sent a little reflected glance round the room, and radiated brightness to the corner.

At last, when it was almost too dark to see even with all these added pinpoints of flame, the outside door was flung open. Tom Garland stood there, with his hand on the latch, bringing a breath of coldness and a flurry of wind. He looked round in astonishment.

"Hadn't you better light up? They've welly finished and here you are sitting like blind men," he said indignantly, and he stamped through the kitchen and passage to the back door for his yokes.

That was the signal and mother and daughter sprang to their feet. Night had stepped down from the hills while they were unaware and it had entered the house.

Mrs. Garland stooped to the fire and lighted a candle. She went to the parlour, where a smouldering slack fire glimmered sleepily on the sideboard and threw queer odd shadows on the walls. Susan glanced quickly at them, and hesitated in the doorway as she listened to their soft sibilant voices. She was glad her mother had entered first. They had been talking together, she knew full well, they had been laughing and running about, playing hide and seek, or enacting some age-old story of love and elope-ment; and now with the entry of the candle they fled behind curtains or rushed into the wall-cupboards. Mrs.

Garland poked the fire, and they made frantic leaps to the ceiling. She pulled the shutters out of the walls by their little black knobs; she straightened their hinged folds with a clatter, and drew them across the window. She lifted an iron bar and let it fall with a clang into the socket. How truly it fitted! How strong was this barrier bound with iron! How safe they were in their little fortress!

Mother smiled at daughter, and each was aware of the other's thoughts, although never a word was spoken.

Susan walked with a lilting step to the second window, which overlooked the yard. As she pulled the shutter across she caught a glimpse of the horse gazing over the stable door with his eyes upon the firelit room. He wanted companionship, he was part of the household, as surely as Susan herself, and she gave him a nod before she shut him out. Invaders were defied, the room was enclosed, there was a feeling of security against all bogeys and robbers who might want to come in. When the shutters were closed and the thick curtains drawn across, a romantic air pervaded the parlour, and Susan looked round with approval at the frisking firelight and the dancing shadows captured and held in the stronghold. There were ancient smells in the room, of wine and rose-leaves and mildew, smells soaked in the furniture and walls, and there were soft sounds, unceasing, the pattering of mice and the rustling of dead leaves and the sighing of the wind in the chimney.

Mrs. Garland turned away, smiling secretly at the memories of old days which twilight evoked in that shadowed room.

"Come along, Susan child. Come to the stone room," she said, but Susan lingered in the half-light, listening to the room calling her. It spoke and she refused to answer. It

86

whispered and she shook her head. It waved its shadow fingers and chattered and muttered but she had nothing to say. She couldn't stop; she dare not stop to listen to all the tales it had to tell. "Another time," she whispered, "another time I'll hear," and she ran across the hall with quick glances at the spirits of the dusk.

Mrs. Garland was already busy in the stone room, at the shutters next to the door, and Susan went to the second window by the gable end. She always chose that casement, for it framed her favourite view. It was very beautiful and mysterious out there in the soft dusk, with the sombre yews close to her face, and the dim lawn under the window, the white gate luring her to the fields, the tall apple-trees alive and vibrant against the evening sky. Beyond them the wooded hill rose abruptly, and on its summit stood the lightning-blasted oak. Susan never tired of staring through that magic casement, to that five-barred gate which led to Paradise. Even as she pressed her nose against the pane her mother finished and clanged the bar of the shutters, and Susan hurried lest she should be left in the darkness.

Every window at the farm had its own peculiar magic for Susan. Each was a peep-hole into some enchanted scene, an eye opened upon the real and unreal world. None was homely or commonplace or dull. Every vista had some strange mysterious content, some secret which might be divulged if Susan were quick to catch it. The dairy window looked out on the water troughs, with the moss-green wall and the filbert trees. If she crept softly up to it she could watch the play of the water from the spring, and the latticed ripples, without the water being aware. She could see the thrush fly down to the trough's edge to drink, and the squirrel leap in a flurry of red from the filbert trees on to the wall. From the parlour window there were the roses that nodded close by, and the garden with its wicket gate. Sometimes the gate opened, and her mother went in for a bunch of carrots, a stick of celery, a spray of parsley, unaware of the still ghostlike face and the brown eyes gazing down at her. Another window looked out to the yard, and this was indeed secret. It was such a peep-hole that it had a linen blind for protection, to keep the servant lad from peering into the room. It overlooked the dog-kennel, with Roger prowling up and down, and the barn with Dan pitching hay from the loft to the manger, or Joshua chopping sticks in the dimness with the big corn bins behind him and the stone bench by his side. The kitchen window opened to the loveliest view of all, hill and valley, and there Susan could see the grey shapes of rain sweep down the fields, she could catch the ghost of the north wind on its ruffling journey over the grass, or watch the hail-stones spring with sudden vehemence out of the winter sky. Great events could be witnessed—the coming of a storm, heralded by black clouds which moved in majesty across the wide sky, the spin of raindrops, the wind moving fleetfoot over the grass, turning it white in its passage. All those remote and grand happenings, snow and sunshine, haloes and lightnings, took place on that hillside beneath the kitchen window.

The lamp was swung from a hook in the ceiling and lighted with a spill. The warm beams of brightness shone out across the fields to the woods. Margaret always left it thus to send its welcoming glow to the men milking in the cowhouses, or to travellers driving in the valley below. That star of light was more than a lamp illuminating a room. It was a symbol of fraternity to strangers and wanderers, an earthly spark answering the stars of heaven, telling God Himself they were down there, living in a little farm on a lonely hillside, reminding Him to take care of them.

Becky set the table for tea, and delicious strong smells of food filled the kitchen. Susan crouched on the hearth and toasted the large home-made teacakes and piled them on the stove. Becky cut thick slices of bread and butter at the table end, where the cloth was folded back. Margaret Garland peeped in the oven at the apples roasting, cracking their skins, spilling their snowy foam. With little cries at their goodness, she brought them out. Susan fetched a jug of cream from the dairy, and a round heavy seedcake from the pantry shelf. Becky scrubbed the white sticks of celery at the sink and arranged them, with green tips and thick sweet hearts, in the fluted glass.

Outside was the deep spacious night. The interior of the room was reflected on the window, but by pressing her face against the pane Susan could see the cowhouses. A little glimmer moved across the cow-yard, and then another star joined it. The two lights bobbed and bowed as if talking together, and then they moved in dancing rhythm like spectral will-o'-the-wisps one behind another across the field path. The men were returning with their brimming milkcans, walking slowly to keep the milk from spilling, swinging the lanterns by their pails.

"They're coming! Quick! Mash the tea! We mustn't keep your father waiting," cried Margaret, and she seized the brown teapot, and held it to the spout of the boiling kettle. All must be ready when the men came to the house.

They clattered into the backyard and jingled the cans as they set them down on the stones by the cooling troughs. Then there was a swish of water, and a cry of "Steady on! Steady on!" as the cans were lowered and swung on the hooks in the water. The servant lad stood outside the window, and his dark eye flashed and his face was like a foreigner's as he unfastened the iron latchets that hooked the shutters to the wall. He swung the creaking doors across and whistled loudly, and Susan went to the window to help. It gave her a strange pleasure to see the reflection of the room as in a mirror, with the cloth on the table, the hanging lamp shining in that other room, the row of terra-cotta jugs on the dresser shelf, and her own pale face staring there at the strange goblin face of the farm lad in the outer blackness. It was a ghost scene, with reflections and reality as in Pepper's famous play at the fair. What could it all mean?

She stood lost in wonder, but Dan frowned and called out to her.

"Come on! I can't wait here all night! Be quick!" and his voice was merged in the noise of running water and clink of pails.

He drew the shutters close to the panes and pushed the iron cotter through the hole in the frame, pressing it close, and stamping his feet with impatience at Susan's efforts to push the stiff pin through the cotter's eye. It was fast at last, and she rapped on the glass, the sign that it was secure. Becky would fasten the dairy shutter on a dark night like this.

The front door was already locked and bolted, and as soon as the outside work was finished the other doors were locked. The great iron keys were put on the dresser end, keys of stable and barn and cowhouses, of brewhouse and cartshed and Irishmen's Place, all were there, massive keys and looped handles shiny with age. The fields and woods were blotted out. No longer could the vagrant and outcast find their way to the house's comfort. The farm was in darkness, completely shut among the trees in a hidden kingdom of its own, safe from marauders as in days of old.

The interior was bright with lamps and candles, with sources of light and reflections. Every brass candlestick on the mantelpiece and copper saucepan on the shelf sent out little points of fire, and the polished surface of the dresser and cupboards seemed to emit their own intrinsic radiance.

After tea chairs were drawn up to the fire, for work and for reading, and the men seated on the left of the fireplace took out their clasp-knives and shaved wood into spills to save matches. The light was gentle, it softened their features, and lay in gold bars on their bent heads. The shadows leaped and bowed on the buff-painted walls, on dish covers and harness and guns, with every movement of the company, so that all the room seemed to be alive.

Margaret took a book from her apron drawer and read aloud, while Becky got on with the rug-making. Pieces of cloth had been collected through many a year, suits left behind by the dead, garments with the worn pieces cut away. They were cut into strips and pegged in a pattern on a background of hessian to make hearthrugs. The finer and better rugs, of soft grey cloths, were sent to the parlour and hall, and gay many-coloured speckled rugs were laid on kitchen and attic floors, to warm cold feet in icy weather, to keep the draughts at bay. It took a whole winter to peg one large rug, and Becky worked at it all her spare time.

The kitchen was a centre of amusement, for there was nothing in the village. A church tea twice a year, a chapel anniversary, and a missionary lecture were the special treats. These were attended with a great preparation, polishing the best lanterns, watching the clock, arranging the comforts of those left behind to guard the house. There was a long walk to the village, with cloaks and lanterns and strong boots and sticks, for Tom Garland seldom took his horse out at night unless there was the rare excitement of a circus or a wild beast show at the little town in the next valley. There was the return in the black night, with the lantern wavering on the ground, and the exquisite sight of the lamp shining through the unshuttered window high among the trees to welcome the travellers and guide them home.

But on ordinary nights there was plenty to do, and Margaret planned long ahead for the winter. Mittens of scarlet wool were knitted for old Joshua, whose hands were badly chapped with frost. Woollen cuffs were ready for all farm workers, and kneecaps were made for aged people who were full of rheumatism.

Ancient dresses that had lain hidden in chests for many years were adapted into something fashionable according to country standards. Sometimes there was an orgy of hat making, especially if someone visited the farm with town notions. Then the most wonderful tam-o'-shanters and toques were invented, and hoods edged with fur and bonnets of velvet. Pheasant-shooting brought hat-trimming, and the iridescent neck feathers were dried for pads after the shooting party had been to the farm.

The bright hot kitchen was the scene of all these activities, for nobody wanted to go to the parlour, to sit in lonely state. Susan drew her low chair up to the table and cut strips of cloth for Becky, while she listened to the reading of *Uncle Tom's Cabin*, or the books of Dickens, or *Robinson Crusoe*. When Margaret was too busy to read Tom Garland entertained the company with tales of long ago.

He told the famous story of the fox-raid upon the farm hen-roost, when the biggest dog fox ever known was tracked across the river and the railway line away to the high woods, and he told of the horse-thief, who stole the mare and would have been hanged "if he had been catched but he wasna. And we lost our grand mare."

Susan made little books of notepaper, and wrote her poems, licking her pencil, and staring round the room at blazing logs and pewter mugs, at dangling hams and printed texts, looking for inspiration in their homely faces.

The clock struck eight, with slow deliberation like a countryman's talk, and they all stopped to listen and count to see that old grandfather hadn't made a mistake. They ate their roast potatoes with bowls of milk and pats of butter, and then Susan prepared for bed. A candle was lighted, and she parted reluctantly from the merry company.

Upstairs was another land, but a fire burned in her bedroom and thick curtains were drawn across. The wind beat on the walls and the flames of the fire danced and quivered in the draught. She lay in bed, watching the shadows again, thin long shades moving over door and curtain, companions for the night. Down below Margaret was reading a romance aloud. It was called *East Lynne*. Soon they would all go to bed and the house would be shrouded inside as well as out. That was the time when all the shadows congregated in the kitchen and lived once again. The house itself awoke, and remembered the past. Susan wanted to listen to the talk of those others, whom nobody else saw, those others who had lived there once. She lay, half asleep, and whispering shadows and the low fire murmured together.

One night Margaret read aloud a story called *The Patchwork Quilt*. It was an old-fashioned serial which had come out in weekly numbers and lain forgotten in a chest. It kept the family entranced, for it contained many tales, one leading to another like those told by Scheherazade to the Sultan in Susan's lamented and beloved *Arabian Nights' Entertainment*, although it lacked the oriental colour and magic of that lost book. A girl lay ill and the fourposter in which she slept was covered with a quilt of patchwork. She questioned her mother about the faded scraps and heard the stories of the people who had once worn them. From the little patches the life of a village community with all its hopes and fears was evolved. It was a fine idea to Susan, for everybody at the farm slept under a quilt which could tell tales. Susan looked with new interest at the cover of her own bed, and she thought of the hundred stories that lay hidden in the flowery hexagons of which it was made.

Ever since she could remember she had seen her mother making these quilts. Margaret's little needle flicked like lightning as she seamed the pieces together. The quilts grew, one for each bed, and a beautiful one which took some years to make was taken upstairs to the chest and folded away for Susan's wedding day. There it lay wrapped in old linen, with scented herbs, bitter and strong, and the paper linings left inside the patches. Susan was allowed to open it out at Christmas. On festal days when relations came the quilt was displayed to the critical eyes of ancient great-aunts.

The quilts had each their own particular design and character. They were rich-man and poor-man, they were grand and homely, they were ready for a bishop's lady or a ploughboy. The quilt for the parlour bedroom was made with hexagons of silk and velvet which Margaret had begged from her friends, and collected since she was a young girl. The quilt for the servant man's bedchamber was a patchwork of oblong pieces of pink and blue and lavender prints from hayfield frocks, padded to make it warm. There were quilts with diamonds and squares, the simpler patterns for common use, the more elaborate for honoured guests.

In the deepest drawer of the old Chippendale sideboard there was a pillow-case filled with scraps of velvet and silk in delicate colours, the blue of forget-me-not, the magenta of petunias, the red of foxgloves. These were for the best patchwork, for cushions and chairs in the parlour. Susan begged to look into this collection, and she touched the soft scraps with reverent fingers as if they were immortal flowers. There were colours she had never seen, and a turquoise blue and a dark purple affected her so strongly that she stole them and kept them for private worship.

Another pillow-case held pieces of cretonne, printed with violets and primroses, with stiff bluebells and rosebuds, and many a device of early Victorian days. She sniffed at them, half expecting to smell the scent of flowers. The odour of the old cretonne was equally ravishing. It was as delicious as country blossoms to her small nose.

A third held prints of many patterns, spotted, pied, striped and chequered, flower-sprinkled and powdered with leaves. There were pieces of Susan's own frocks and her mother's, left over from the making, together with scraps of brocade and silk tartan ribbon, finery of people long dead, collected for many a year before she was born. They lay in the deep drawer, clean and bright, pervaded by a queer ancient fragrance, of musk and orris-root and closed spaces, faint mildew and drapery shops.

With them was a pile of papers, cut in regular shapes of hexagons and diamonds, from letters, sermons, hymn sheets. It was stiff paper, some of it crossed and recrossed with crabbed writing, envelopes with the latticed red stamps of the seventies.

There Susan read sacred poems, and homilies, and recipes for long-forgotten salves: "1 ounce Ipec. The *Jouice* of a Lemon. A pinch of rue," and, "*Through all the changing scenes of life,*" each cut to shape.

The scraps of silk were securely tacked over the paper patterns, ready for the quilts. Myriads of these little flower-like discs were prepared by Margaret and her friends on winter nights. There was usually someone to keep the farm company through the long dark months when they were cut off from society. Relations came for a month or two, unpaid helpers joined the circle, and they were welcomed with joy, to share the evening games, the reading aloud and the quilt-making. There was dour Sarah Jane, who prophesied the end of the world; and quick, sprightly Trot, who wore a tartan brooch and told Susan about her native Scotland; and ancient Mrs. Tibbet, who wore a lace cap and drank camomile tea every night. As the women worked Margaret read aloud a chapter or two of Dickens, with little glances to see that all was going correctly.

When sufficient patches had been covered Margaret fitted them together and sewed with the smallest of stitches, making a pattern with the complicated web spread out over her white apron. Everyone was dazzled by the ingenuity she displayed in her arrangement of the colours, for she balanced the tones and kept the rainbow hues subdued. There were perspectives too, of rhomboids and circles, interlacing and framing a design.

When the quilt was large enough, after many months' work, the stiffening papers were removed and the tacking threads taken out. A padded lining was fitted, made from layers of soft old blankets, and sheep's wool from the flock. The quilt was backed with a piece of new material bought from the town, crimson merino for a best bed, red Turkey twill for common use. Then it was bound with its matching cord, and it was ready for use.

As Margaret sewed, Susan handed her the little coloured pieces from her apron and she questioned her about their origin. Margaret sighed and shook her head.

"This little pattern is from my sister Eliza's Sunday dress. It was pale blue taffeta with a silk fringe, and she wore it over a crinoline. How lovely she looked in it! I was only a child, for I was the youngest, like your father, but I remember very well. She died when she was twenty-one. She fell in a decline and just faded away."

Margaret gave a deep sigh, and Susan stared, uneasy in her mind, wondering if she too was doomed to such an

end at twenty-one. Everybody seemed to die in a decline
or to gallop in consumption and she thought of those
young girls of mid-Victorian days, running swiftly with
white faces down the steep slope to the grave.

"There's another piece of one of her dresses," Margaret
continued, unaware of the haunting fears in Susan's mind,
and she searched among the scraps for a slip of brown
velvet.

"This was her winter dress. Poor Eliza! It had brown
acorns down the front, and she had a muff made of the
same velvet. She was the very image of you, Susan."

Susan frowned and pointed to a segment of crimson silk.

"What was this?" she demanded quickly, and Margaret
changed her sighs to laughter.

"That was a bit of a petticoat I once had. Not that I could
afford such a thing as a silk petticoat, for they *were* silk in
those days, they stood up of themselves and nearly walked
alone! But this was left me by my Aunt Tabitha. 'My best
quilted petticoat of crimson silk to my niece Margaret,' said
she, and I wore it for ten years. When you were born I cut
it up and some of it made a cushion cover and some a
bonnet for you. You looked sweet in that crimson quilted
bonnet with a lace frill next to your cheeks."

Susan sighed for past glories, for her clothes were drab
and serviceable.

"This is a piece of my Aunt Susan's dress," continued
Margaret, touching with lingering fingers a diamond of
black watered silk. "She promised to leave me a hundred
pounds in her will, for I was the one who looked after her.
I did all her sewing, for I was reckoned to be clever with
my fingers. I read aloud to her, for her eyes were weak and
she liked my voice. I would have done anything for her,
poor soul, for I loved her so. 'A hundred pounds I'll leave

you,' she whispered with secret chuckles. Her own daughters were proud and well-married, and they cared nothing for her. I didn't want to take the money, for I loved her for herself, but it cheered her in those last months to think she was giving it, and she used to talk with me about how I should spend it."

Margaret bent her head over the quilt and her needle flew in and out as she talked. Susan stroked the watered silk, listening eagerly.

"'You buy a new plough for Thomas, and a hay chopper and a little horse, if the money will run to it,' said my aunt, knowing nothing of the cost of farm things. I was just getting married at the time. 'A little horse to gallop along the roads. And perhaps a new cart. And a dress for yourself, my dear, and some left to put in the bank.'

"Then she would murmur in her weak voice. 'Just a little horse. Perhaps a young colt if a horse costs too much. A little foal. Just a little small foal.' She lay back imagining that horse, seeing him in her mind's eye running up and down the fields, galloping to market, her little horse!

"Your father shook his head when I told him. 'They won't let her. They'll take everything, mark my words,' said he."

"And did you get the horse?" Susan asked eagerly.

"She made her will all right," Margaret answered slowly. "But when she died there was nothing for me, not a locket or a prayer-book. They found out about the legacy and made her tear it up. She wept about it to me, and I comforted her, saying I should remember till life's end, and I only wanted a trifle she had touched. So when she was gone I begged for a scrap of one of her dresses, which they were cutting up, and this is part of it."

99

There was silence. Margaret thinking of the old woman, dominated by those others, imprisoned in her bed, Susan rubbing her finger over the watered silk, with its ripples like the river.

"And you never bought the new plough, and the hay cutter, and the little horse and cart, and the best dress, Mother?" she asked, in a sad whisper.

"No. The money would have been a God-send to us, for we had hard trials. But we pulled through and here we are!"

So she went on with her tales, unromantic stories, unlike those in the tattered book. It was ordinary everyday life, with birth and death, marrying and having children, and no excitements like runaway matches and highwaymen. It wasn't the kind of life Susan was going to have, and she decided she would make her own tales where nobody died. There was a patch of ruby satin for the doublet of the king's eldest son, and when he married the goose-girl she was dressed in the patch of silk with the embroidered nosegays sprinkled upon it. She fitted the patterns into all the fairy tales she had ever read, and told them to herself as she lay in the wooden bed with the firelight glinting on the little hexagons that covered her with their web of fantasy.

Going Down with the Milk

Of all the joyful experiences in childhood and later in youth, this going down with the milk was the one we craved the most. Not only my brother and I but everybody under the age of seventeen who came to stay with us, wanted to go down with the milk.

It was a privilege granted on certain occasions, of necessity a Saturday or a holiday pleasure. Usually only one person was allowed to accompany the driver, as the cart had its load of milk churns, and it was unfair to give the stalwart brown pony too heavy a load. There were arguments and prayers about this delectable journey, and secret tears were shed, but nothing could change my father when he said no. We might as well save our breath to cool the porridge waiting for us in shallow blue dishes with a jug of cream to pour over it.

The one who had been down returned with bright eyes and glowing cheeks, excited and happy, with tales to tell and the air of an intrepid traveller. He carried a bird's egg, a bunch of wild roses, a pebble, and he brought in with him a powder of pollen and seeds and sweet odours of the lanes. It was a great adventure, a gift to childhood, for the very young were preferred to the older ones, not only because their anticipation was greater but because their weight was less and they could squeeze on the seat without a reproachful glance from the pony.

It was all so simple, so ordinary, to adult minds, but to us it was the quintessence of bliss. A day begun with "going

down with the milk" was eternally blessed whatever happened to the rest of the twenty-four hours. It was something
plucked from eternity, never to be forgotten, a ride
through the gardens of Paradise. For it was Paradise indeed
early in the morning, with the dew on the grass and the
sunlight shining through the beech wood, falling through
the smooth trunks in parallel lines, to bar with black and
gold the path along which we drove. Every flower and leaf
seemed to glow with an inner illumination of its own, which
was discovered to us, as we took quick glances down from
the seat. The call of the cuckoo like a warm-toned bell
through the milky-white mists of early morning, the cry of
the pheasant, the sound of the mowers in the fields, all were
the music of the journey. We drove down from our own
high clear air to the soft curling wreaths which dissolved as
the sun went up the sky, and that was a joy to witness. A
sign of hot weather, they said, but we felt elated as we saw
this milky cloud below us, in the days of summer.

The railway line, which curved in a wide sweep following
the contour of the valley between the wooded hills, was
quite romantic to our eyes, and I was always fascinated as I
stared from the Daisy Bank through the tops of the apple
trees at the little trains that ran smoothly as clockwork toys
with their white banners of smoke floating behind, alongside the river. Even the shapes assumed by the smoke were
something to wonder at, and we always counted the trucks
in the "luggage-trains", which moved with great solemnity
and deliberation and sudden clatters and reverses. The
passenger trains were infrequent, and we knew them all
and compared their passing with our grandfather clock.

The scene had such a hold on my imagination that I have
never lost the exhilaration of watching trains. Everything
connected with a train had its own peculiar interest not only

to myself but to everyone else, partly because our livelihood was bound up with the railway that took our milk to the towns, but also because we looked at it from the point of view of travellers who seldom travelled.

We liked trains, we admired them. At night we saw the golden dragon of glittering fire reflected in the river and when we stood by the orchard wall looking at the immensity of the sky, waiting for a shooting star to fall down the heavenly blue, then we also saw the earthly meteor speeding in the blackness of the valley.

The train came out of a tunnel in the hill at a sudden bend of the river, and it crossed the waters, echoing and rumbling with a deep note on the iron bridge. It ran along the valley by the river, on the embankment raised above meadows full of wild geraniums and dog-daisies, and it crossed the river again above the rocks and leaping water and dipping trees, to puff to a standstill at our little station. It always seemed surprised to arrive there. Then it entered a long sulphurous tunnel under the ridge crowned by fields, and was lost to our view.

There was one train above all others that we regarded as a friend, almost a relation, even as our own intimate possession. It was the milk train, that dark sturdy little slow-coach that carried the milk from farms in the valleys round about for many miles.

Every morning at 7·53 it arrived, and was loaded up with milk churns, sweet new milk from the hill and valley farms. Every night it came back with empty churns which it tossed out on the platform with a tinkling clangour like a score of anvils, and it took in the night milk. At each station down the line it was the same. It chugged along the valley, often very late. It had a voice of its own, and a whistle of its own, and a rumbling gait and a slow ambling motion, as if it enjoyed the journey, as I have no doubt it did, for it was a true countryman in the world of trains. It waited for late passengers, and the guard used to lean over the palings at the station to beckon people who were hurrying up the steps. It knew all the travellers and missed them if they were not ready.

About the same time, morning and evening, a milk train went in the opposite direction, also laden with churns. The up and down trains were like twins, and as the churns of milk had to be rolled over the railway line at a crossing or dragged in milk-barrows by the farm men, everything had to be ready before the two trains arrived. So one had the felicity of seeing two trains when one went down with the milk, two lots of passengers and two engines, with only a few minutes between. This eight o'clock rendezvous was the supreme moment of the day, for station-master, for porters and all of us. At night when the empty churns came back, and only a few farmers sent their milk, the thrill had gone. Nobody wanted to leave haymaking, or cricket, or tea on the grass-plat to go down to the station. The glory had departed, it had moved to the hill-top, to the sunny pastures and farm buildings, and the little station and tired old train were dusty and in shadow.

Those who went down with the milk had to be dressed neatly, washed and brushed, breakfasted and ready by twenty minutes past seven in the morning, and not a minute late. The house was full of bustle and commotion. The doors were wide open and great cans of milk, holding many gallons, were carried through the kitchen on yokes, from the water troughs where they had been hanging for half an hour after their preliminary cooling in the troughs at the farm buildings.

Going Down with the Milk

There were clean fresh sounds in the early morning, the silvery tinkle of milk cans ringing like bells on the stones, of water running through the milk-cooler fixed to the house wall, of the spring bubbling into the great stone troughs, and the thud of the pump sending water from the underground spring to the milk-cooler. The water ran out and dripped down the hill-side on the moss and nettles and stonecrop. There was the ring of the horse's hooves in the stony yard, and the jingle of the harness and bell. Somebody ran out with a kettle, and put it on the flat, smooth, well-scrubbed paving stones by the troughs. The lading-can was swished backward and forward over the drinking water to scatter the floating leaves and flower petals from the damson tree above it. The clear cold water was brought up in this dipper and poured into the kettle. I was usually there with a hazel stick, to stir the milk and watch the cooler at work. Round and round went my slender wand, very clean and smooth, and the warm milk swirled in a hollow inverted cone as I stirred it. Then, for the joy of it, I dropped a few milky spots on the water in the next trough, and watched them fall in the translucent depths, reflecting the picture of myself and the blue sky and the little leaves of the damson tree.

The horse had to be caught, and the one who went down with the milk usually helped with this ticklish but exciting business. He had been turned into the croft or orchard the night before to make the catching easy, but even in the small green enclosure he would gallop and prance, and there was a seductive move towards him with a wooden scoop of oats held in one hand and the halter behind the back, ready to slip over his head. One of us could be useful to aid the harassed lad, by turning the horse when he galloped with flying heels. So there we stood, with arms outstretched, heart beating loudly, as the animal snorted and swung away. The sunlight fell on his shining flanks, his eyes glittered, he was a heroic horse as he bore down on us, and I was not a very brave stone-waller. When he was caught and taken to the stable, the halter removed and the bridle put on, there was a hurried breakfast, eaten standing. Even the food tasted different. The hot toast, with beef dripping filling its crannies and a sprinkle of salt on the top, the tea with cream floating on it, was food fit for the gods.

The stable door was open, and the glittering morning sunshine flooded the bits of straw and the manger, gilding the stone floor. The door of the cart-shed was flung wide and the horse was backed into the spring cart. Martins flew in and out of their nests over the doorway, twittering with excitement, as he came slipping and clattering down the stony slope. Again he was backed with many admonitions, and "Whoa" and "Whey" and "Steady there", into the milk-loading place. This was a cutting in the rocky yard, just wide enough to hold the cart, and it was lined and edged with stonewalling. It was one of our favourite places for games, a den for hide-and-seek, a jumping pitch, the best situation for playing house.

The milk had been measured and the notes put inside the lids and the churns locked. The back of the cart was let down on its hinges, and it was easy for the men to roll the heavy churns on their iron rims along the narrow paved path to the stone sill and into the cart. One man could do it while the other held the horse's head, to keep the cart steady against the wall. The horse moved forward and the back of the cart was fastened with two iron pins which hung on chains. All was ready for the journey and my father took his big silver turnip watch from his waistcoat pocket and held it in the palm of his hand with the double chain dangling, and then he looked at the grandfather clock, and then he went out to survey the sky once more, as if to be quite sure of God's time.

The servant boy, who had been drinking a basin of hot tea with many deep breaths to cool it, and many noisy sips, now came out of the kitchen with the whip. The horse glanced around to see if everybody was ready, for he knew full well all about the milk train. He was as eager as we to start the journey. The small passenger ran out and climbed into the cart.

"Time to be off," cried my father, looking at his watch again.

The seat was readjusted in its socket as the churns took up so much room. We glanced round at the house, at our mother, waving her hand, at the dog dancing up and down, at my father, standing there hatless. We were off! The servant boy walked down the hill, leading the horse. The slope was so steep that we seemed to lean over the horse's haunches. His feet slithered, the cart swayed and rocked as violently as a ship in a storm, and the lad held firmly to the horse's head.

Foxgloves nodded at us, nearly touching our faces, from the banks between which we rode. The scent of gorse and honeysuckle and wild roses filled the air, and we breathed it in, intensely aware of its sweetness, which was mingled with the strong odour of the horse. These smells were all part of life, of going down with the milk. We put out a hand to steady the churns rattling behind us, and we held on to the warm friendly wood of the cart, old and smooth as ivory, polished like furniture which has been in a house for a hundred years.

Now and then the lad would run a few steps ahead and

pick up an enormous stone which some careless person had thrown from the wall. He put it on the grass verge, ready for the return journey, when there would be time to replace it in the wall. Each stone knocked out left a gap like a missing tooth, and we patiently put back these broad-shaped stones, lifting them with two hands, fitting them into the wall.

Sometimes we met a wandering cow or a couple of startled calves down the lane, and our task was to drive the animals safely into the field. The servant boy opened the gate and held it wide while we drove through, proudly holding the reins, guiding the horse safely past the stone posts, and then pulling him up as the lad shut the gate and leapt up to the cart. He took the whip to speed down the field road. There was another gate farther along, a lovely gate in its great bank of musky wild roses, so that I tried to snatch a few flowers, leaning from the cart side, as we passed.

There was much to see, to smell, to know about, birds in the trees, a spring in the field, a trickle of water rising from the earth singing as it ran through the grass, a group of wild blue geraniums, the descendants of which now bloom in my southern garden.

Down the steep hill, under the arching trees which made a shade like green water, went the horse with clattering hooves, dislodged stones rolling after him, and we held tightly to the cart. He went between high banks of many flowers, shining red, yellow and blue in the tall grasses, where red campion, yellow archangel and bluebells grew. The air was cool and heavy scented—garlic and nettles and goose-grass mingling with the sweetness of the bluebells. The difficulties were over, the horse began to trot even before he reached the bottom of the hill as if rejoicing that there was the prospect of a level piece of good road under his feet. The cart swayed dangerously on the sudden curve and then we came to the river for company and the white road and the valley.

The wheels rolled over the stones, rocking the cart sideways, the horse's hooves went click! click! click! That rhythm of four hooves, and the two heavy wheels crunching the stones, was an integral part of one's life. There was the sound of the little bell on the harness and the jingle of chains and creak of leather. The river chuckled and sucked at the stones in its bed, the birds sang gloriously. The cart bumped up and down with its heavy load, shaking our young bones, but we only laughed as we were flung about, swayed this way and that. It was all part of the dazzling excitement of going down with the milk.

We drove along the white dusty road, with the hedge on one side, and on the other the low wall with its incrustations of yellow stonecrop, ferns and little purple toad-flax, and we looked at the river, watching for a kingfisher or a water-hen, pointing at the tossing waters that foamed and tumbled over the shining rocks with a sound that rivalled the hoof beats of the horse and the rattle of the wheels.

It was a different journey from that which we took when my father drove us to the villages. He always spoke in a lilting way to the horse: "Come along, Teddy. Come along." His voice was soothing, reassuring, and the horse's ears twitched as he listened, for the words had a mesmeric effect. Only the other day I heard a man in the Buckinghamshire town where I live, apostrophise his little mare, "Come along, my little old lady. Come along."

The servant boy drove the milk cart; it was part of his daily work, and he had no endearments. The horse had to gallop, so that there was time for a gossip before the trains came in.

I held on to my hat as the wind swept through me, and the heavy churns rocked and banged together. The young man stood up, urging the horse on, as we sped past the square white Georgian house, with its lawns dipping to the road. I knew our friends there were listening to the gallop as they breakfasted in the long dining-room, and shaking their heads over the breakneck speed.

There was a grand roar of sound as we and the river went under the railway bridge, and we always shouted to hear the echo. We swept round the corner, and trotted up the slope to the station, for it was imperative we should enter the station yard in good style, trotting to show off before the others. It was a gesture, a proud entry.

The station approach was decked with flowery banks where grew crimson may, and laburnum, purple lilac and barberry. There was an enclosure with palings around it, where we dragged our hoop sticks to make a musical sound, and we always looked at these brightly coloured trees with admiration, and real enjoyment of the flowers. Workmen with rush baskets climbed over a fence and ran down a narrow path among the bushes to catch the train, on an ancient path that was later closed.

We were proud of the little station, and I thought it was of great importance in the affairs of the world. I liked the buff-painted roof with a small cupola and the room with lattice windows, and the clean little platform, which seemed a part of the station-master's cottage behind the garden hedge.

Every milk cart had its own resting-place in the station yard, and the horses trotted to their places and waited there, facing the steep hill slope with its grass and flowers. We drew up near the station gates, in our time-honoured place. The backs of the carts were lowered, and boys brought the milk barrows for the churns. They helped each other, and when a load was ready it was wheeled down the platform, across the line to the opposite side, two pulling the handles with laughter and talk, the others pushing in the rear. The men and boys chatted together, sharing their experiences, hearing the latest news, and I gazed with interest at their rubber collars, striped with blue and pink, like candy.

I went on the platform to see the sights—a calf in a sack, lying on the ground, wanting some comfort, passengers buying their tickets, calling through the little hole in the wall, dealers with their sticks in their hands, and, best of all, the tunnel. If I leaned forward I could see a tiny circle of light at the far end, and this was a very exciting thing, with its strange perspective, as though I were looking through the wrong end of a telescope. From the tunnel came strange, clanking, ghostly noises, as if a man in chains lived there, and I always associated *The Count of Monte Cristo* with this dark subterranean prison. Sometimes men walked out, carrying lanterns, as if they had been exploring, and I thought how brave they were. Above the tunnel trees were growing, and cattle feeding, and once I walked in the fields and saw a round hole from which the smoke came, like a volcano.

There was a visit to the station-master's office, where the stout little man took the milk tickets, turning between times to attend to the travellers, whose faces peered through the grill. There was always a peep in the porters' little room, where the station lamps were filled with oil, and sometimes a dog was labelled. Usually a group of farm lads stood near, talking of cricket or football according to the season. We had two porters, called Big Porter and Little Porter, the tall man perpetually aggrieved, the Little Porter a cheery, agreeable boy.

I entered the waiting-room to sit for a minute on the horse-hair armchair, to turn the pages of the Bible on the table, and to look in the mirror over the mantelpiece, where I saw a startled excited reflection of myself standing on tiptoe.

When the express dashed through the station, drawing after it a whirl of leaves and bits of straw, I stood back against the platform seat, lest I should be swept away with it. I always longed to put a penny on the line to see if it were flattened, but although I crept to the edge with my penny there was no chance of getting down to the rails; the porters were always watching.

Above the station on the grassy hill overlooking the platform stood the cottage of the station-master with its little garden running down the slope, and the gate opening on to the platform. We could see his wife shake the cloth after breakfast, sending the crumbs to the birds. It was a homely gesture we enjoyed, part of the life of the railway. Sometimes we saw the station-master come from his kitchen, in a great hurry for the train, and his little boy stood there waving to him.

There was great excitement when the train came in, and the guard walked up and down, with his green flag under his arm. He wore a different flower in his buttonhole every day, winter and summer, and the station-master, too, had a posy of sweet peas or roses.

Nearly every station on the line had a small flower-bed or two, filled with pansies, sweet williams and snap-dragons. There was rivalry between these charming little gardens, and a prize was offered for the best. Later, when I went to school by the milk train, and came back on it at night, I joined in the admiration or condemnation of all the small gardens we passed on the journey, and I saw the porters working in them, making a pleasurable scene. Particularly we praised the name of the station made in flowers, in "white rock" (which was arabis), or in lobelia. Our own station was under a cloud, with few flowers except at the approach and I always felt sorry for this.

We liked the red velvet of the railway coach seats, and the woven letters M.R., which later became L.M.S. The letters were a symbol for me, like England, or the Empire and God. We liked the heavy footwarmers, three or four of which were in each carriage to warm our feet in winter. If the foot-warmers were cold, the porter changed them for hot ones.

We used the waiting-room in the distant station in the evening to do our homework while we waited for the milk train to take us home. There was a splendid fire burning, and the porter always came in with buckets of coal with which he made an even greater blaze. We drew the armchairs round the hearth, got out our leather safety ink bottles, and made a little home in the cosy room which we had to ourselves, while the snow fell and the bitter winds blew, and the horses stood in the station yard, under their blankets and rugs, waiting for the late train.

When the morning train trundled away, with clang and clamour, with the waving of the green flag and waving of hands, and shouts of good-bye, we slowly went back to the cart, and waited for the lad to bring the empty churns. The excitement was over, the drive back had none of the rapture of the rapid gallop for the train, but it held a deep satisfaction. There was no urgency about it, the horse ambled slowly until he reached our hill, when he suddenly remembered his stable and speeded up by himself. We got out and walked, in honour bound, gathering flowers, looking for the bird's nest we had spied on the way down, putting the stones on the walls, opening and shutting gates, stopping wistfully to gaze back at the lovely river in the valley, and the railway line. In the gorse bush was the nest of the white-throat which could be looked at on the return home. In the field was a wasps' nest, at which we threw stones and ran away before we were stung. Later the servant boy would go down with brown paper and smoke it out, and sell the nest to a fisherman for a shilling.

We stored up these impressions in our minds, tales to tell, things we had seen on the journey and at the station. The horse, with bent head, and reins tied in a knot to the brake, walked swiftly uphill, with nobody near him. He needed no guidance, he was going home.

We walked up the grassy slope alongside the cart track, among the wild roses and the creamy yarrow, which filled the air with aromatic fragrance. Even in winter we found lovely things on the morning's ride, for icicles were as exquisite as roses, and snow archways hung across the lane.

The dog began to bark, dancing wildly as he heard us; my father stood on the bank looking down at us, and we waved to him; old Josiah was at the stable door. We climbed the steps, and ran to the house, hurrying like the horse going to his stable. There was a rumble of wheels, a shaking of bells, and jingle of empty churns, and the horse and cart appeared suddenly round the corner with the lad behind.

The journey was done, we had been down with the milk, and we had our experiences to relate to my smiling mother. We had gained a day, something precious to carry with us for ever. We each brought back a cargo of sensations and experiences. The servant boy whistled a new song, "The Honeysuckle and the Bee" or "Daisy, Daisy, give me your answer do".

My brother brought back cricket scores, and the names of famous players, Ranji, W. G. Grace, C. B. Fry, Archie MacLaren, with tales of their prowess, records broken and matches won.

I carried a load of secret things, flowers and birds and water, the harsh and bitter smells of sulphur or dog-daisies or smoke, the colour of birds' eggs and the flight of butterflies and bumble-bees.

I was radiant with happiness, for nobody could take away my day, and I sat down for a second breakfast.

Bathrooms

A new house was built on a hillside commanding views across the country. A narrow field under the wood on a far slope had been sold to a retired manufacturer who was coming to live among us with his family of eight children and servants. Never before within living memory had such a thing happened. Nobody ever built a house. The Squire owned nearly all the land, and he wished to keep his villages free from outsiders. Perhaps a cottage had appeared a hundred years ago, built for a workman on the estate, but nothing had been put up since.

From our top pastures, through a gap in the intervening woods we could see the red brick house slowly rising in a forest of scaffolding. It was hidden from us unless we climbed the fields, so we went out to gaze at it. When we fetched the cows for milking, when we went mushrooming, or nutting, or haymaking, we tried to get a glimpse of the distant brightly coloured mansion, and we conjectured about the people who would live there. We wondered how the Squire felt about a vermilion house in a countryside of stone.

Houses had always seemed to be part of the landscape, unobtrusive and unremarked. They fitted into the natural line of hill and valley, they were made of local materials, from stone in the quarries near. They were weathered by the storms and painted by the seasons, till they resembled the earth. Green mosses on the roofs, grey stone walls and gables, silver lichens on the garden walls, they were part of the land. If built on a hill top, they were sheltered by a wood or group of trees. In the valleys they nestled low down into the bosom of the fields, crouching against the warm earth. Little streets of stone cottages clambered among the rocks, and faded into the grey of the roads. Lonely farms were concealed among the orchards and woods. Even the largest houses were lost in the green shade of yew hedges and shadowy hollows. So we looked with surprise at this red house appearing in our quiet country like a flamboyant visitor. It was about three miles away, and when we went to the village shops we made excuses to drive further through the rocky valley to the little town so that we could look up at the monster new house towering above the road.

There were rumours in plenty, but the one that caused the greatest sensation among the villagers was that the house was going to have fourteen bathrooms. Some even said sixteen bathrooms. Fourteen bathrooms, one to each bedroom! Who ever heard the like?

"By Guy! They mun be dirty folk!" cried old Sam Steeples to my father, and we all agreed. It was stupendous. It was beyond our comprehension! Never had anybody heard of such a thing. Even at Windsor Castle there couldn't be fourteen bathrooms, we said. Fourteen, fifteen, sixteen bathrooms, the idea of it amazed us.

The effect upon me was a kind of fairytale wonder. Arabian Nights' Entertainment couldn't do more. If they had had a genie in a bottle to perform miracles for their pleasure; if they had brought a wishing-table that magically set itself with every variety of food; if they had possessed an invisible cloak and Aladdin's lamp, I shouldn't have been surprised, but fourteen bathrooms was too much even for my imagination.

"It fair beats the band! Whatever do they want with all that washing?" asked our servant girl. "They won't have time to do 'owt else except wash themselves if they use them all."

None of us disbelieved the rumour, which was confirmed by the workmen who were putting in the bathrooms. To this day I do not know how true it was, and whether there were fourteen or sixteen.

Everyone took a certain pride that such a thing could happen, and we led visitors to our top pasture and pointed out the wonder, as if it were a palace grown up in the night.

"Do you see that red mark on yonder hill? That's a house with fourteen bathrooms in it."

We debated where the water was coming from to fill those baths. No wonder they had built the house near the river. The green swirling waters flowed in the valley and dropped in a white cascade over the horseshoe weir. We thought there must be some pumping arrangement to supply the baths, for there was no spring such as we enjoyed. It was the talk of the villages, and with clicking of tongues we expressed our surprise that folk who did no work could be so dirty as to need all that bathing. And the coal and wood it would take to get the water hot! And the soap they would use! There was no end to the discussions about those fourteen bathrooms. Marble pavements, said some, for they had seen polished marble carried up the hill.

I had never seen a bathroom, but I could imagine one. I sat on the short soft turf of the Top Pasture, with lady-slipper and milkwort sprinkling the grass at my feet, and the sheep nibbling near me, and I gazed at the faraway house, and thought of those rooms of watery splendour. I dreamed of those bathrooms of fairytale beauty, green river-water flowing from bronze mouths of dragons, blue-silver water shooting up and falling in a cascade to deep baths. There was a little fountain at the fishpond in the yard of the coaching-stable, and I fashioned the bathrooms from that silvery ripple, which held a rainbow in its water-drops.

Different people had different ways of washing. The Irishmen bathed in a bucket, in the croft round the corner among the rocks and rose bushes. Sunday was their bathing day, and they religiously chose their time before they went to Mass. Sometimes I caught a glimpse of their ablutions, as they stood with their trousers tied round their middles, and soaped their hairy chests and dowsed their rough heads, and dried themselves on a roller towel that was passed from one to another. Then they disappeared altogether in the bushes where it was not seemly to look at them. There they changed their trousers and put on clean shirts, and appeared smiling and clean. Afterwards they washed their dirty shirts, and hung them on the haw-thorns and nut bushes to dry. The young handsome Patrick and Dominick borrowed my father's shaving box with his razors and soap, and they carried a little square looking-glass out to the grass plat. They shaved themsel-ves in the sweet fresh air, with birds singing and daisies thick under their bare feet. It was a nice way to bath, out there in the open.

We had no bathroom, nor had anyone else whom I knew, but we had baths. We possessed a fine collection of these, ranging from large flat round baths, which took up most of the floor surface of the little bedrooms, to high-backed oval baths, standing on four legs. They were white inside and grained brown and yellow outside, and very beautiful I thought they were. In the hay-barn next door to the cow-house was a hundred-year-old bath, very high, and long and narrow, like a sarcophagus. It was filled with Indian corn for the fowls, and we leaned perilously over the side with a dipper to draw up the maize, which lay like golden water in the white enamelled interior.

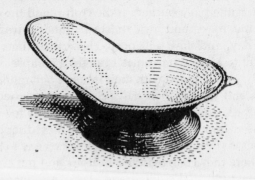

The largest hip bath, with a high moulded back and a hooded spout for emptying the water, was kept in the parlour bedroom for the use of the quality who sometimes honoured us. In the little bedroom which had lately been the cheese-chamber, a small bath was used, a square high tub with four legs. One sat down very carefully lest it should overbalance and the contents flood the carpet. It was the warmest bath, for its sides kept away all draughts.

The smallest bath was one left to us by a canon. The delightful old church dignitary used to stay with us for several weeks each year to compose his sermons and write his books. He brought his painted bath, a little chair and diminutive table with him. We kept them ready for his visits. When, after many years, he died, they were part of his bequest to us, and the little bath went with me to London.

These painted, polished baths that inhabited our house were familiar as human beings, and I felt a strong affection for them. I knew their idiosyncrasies—which bath was chilly and safe, which was warm but unsteady. One of them needed a great deal of water, so it was unpopular, and another was difficult to empty without spilling.

There was a humbler bath which was kept in the back kitchen for the occasional use of farm workers. The servant man carried it to his loft and bathed in it. The servant girl had her bath before the kitchen fire on Saturday nights when everyone had gone to bed. It was my own bath when I was very young, and it was a washtub too. It was called "The Tin Pancheon", a dignified name, for it was round and high and large. I fitted into it like a snail in a shell, hidden by its high walls. The wide house doors were open to the yards, and the wind came rushing through the house nearly sweeping the naked bather out of the water.

A bath night was additional work for the servant girl but everyone was used to carrying water. A milk-can was filled from the drinking-water trough among the ferns and borne icy-cold to the bedroom. Another milk-can holding several gallons was half-filled with hot water from the kitchen copper-pan. A bath sheet of great size and thickness was spread over the carpet and there were warning cries, "Keep away! Are you ready?" as the bath was filled.

The steam circled in ghostly eddies, and the candle paled in the haze. In winter there was always a good fire alight on the bedroom hearth, and the bath was placed near. There one sat in the greatest contentment, with the dancing flames in the chimney, with the candle sending grotesque enormous shadows on the closely drawn tapestry curtains, and the cake of Pears' soap mingling its own intimate smell with the strong aromatic odour of the hot rain-water. That water came from the enormous wooden vats under the roof edge, where generations of elm leaves had fallen and decayed. The smell was a rich one, compounded of ferns and moss and vegetation. The woodland birds which bathed in the pools deep among the trees must have had the same kind of leafy smell as they splashed. A bath without that autumnal smell was no bath. And the softness of the water! It was like silk as it poured from the sponge and splashed over the sides to the floor. So there one sat, dreaming by the fire, unconscious of time, staring at the gold caverns and castles in the flames, listening to the wind as it beat against the strong walls of the farmhouse, and the creaking of the shutters and the cries of the owls. There one sat, blissfully naked, burning at the front, freezing at the back, dripping the hot water over one's body. Nobody knocked at the bathroom door, for it was private property. Nobody wanted to come in. The water could remain there till morning, when the servant girl would come after milking with her cans and carry it away, groaning over the weight, remarking that it wasn't worth having a bath if you couldn't make the water dirtier than that!

The water would be carried downstairs, through the kitchen, and used to swill the stone paths. In summer it would go to the rose trees and soak the roots of the Glory roses, or the cabbage roses on the old building. It wouldn't be wasted. There was a continuity about life, which made me part of all things, of water and trees and rain, and the bath-water soaked back into the earth, its home.

On the slender mahogany towel-rail beside the fire, sheltering the bath from the door, hung a bath-towel, as big as a sheet. It was one of the ancient towels which had been in the oak chest on the landing for fifty years before I was born. There in the corner was the date to prove it. It had the smell of lavender, and tansy, and camomile, sweet and bitter herbs strewed there, and also the smell of Pears' which was stored in the chest. The scent of that chest was so strong that everything inside was permeated with it, and it saturated the bath-towels. I dried by the fire, and slipped over my head my warm calico nightgown adorned with feather-stitching on its turned-down collar. Then a dash to the door, and out to the dark landing to call and call, to ring a brass bell, and call again, every moment getting colder, for there were no dressing-gowns or luxuries.

Noises came from downstairs, deep voices talking, rumbling laughter, somebody singing, the grandfather clock striking and drowning all else, chairs grating on stone floors, and outside a cow mooing in the Irishman's Place. At last my voice was heard, and a beam of light appeared.

Upstairs came my mother bearing a bowl of steaming bread and milk with a sprinkle of brown sugar, and nutmeg and thick cream on the top. That was to keep me from catching cold after the exposure of my bath.

I scrambled into the wide bed with its three or four feather mattresses piled so high that I sank into them as if into a snow-drift.

In that cold bed with its heavy old linen sheets was a hotwater bottle of ancient lineage. It was the alternative to the copper warming-pan which hung on the kitchen wall. Hot bricks were heated in the oven for a couple of hours and then wrapped in scraps of blanket for the servant men and girls, but this was the oldest bottle in the house, for it dated from the early years of the nineteenth century. It was made of copper, with rounded sides and flat base. The screwed stopper was of brass, and as the expansion of the two metals differs, the bottle was airtight. This brought about a curious phenomenon. In the middle of the night, when the bottle was cooling, a singing began, as the water boiled under decreased pressure. Ever shriller and sweeter was the sound, until in the morning a symphony of strange music came from the hot-water bottle. It was a friendly homely noise, very companionable in a lonely room, but startling to a stranger who thought that birds and mice were warbling in the bed.

The lighted candle was placed on the little oak table by the bedside, a story book near it. I ate my bread and milk with glances at the queer shadows which moved around the room. The round wooden balls on the bed posts were the same size as my head, and their shadows bobbed alongside in a ghostly manner, as the firelight rose and fell.

I put my candle closer and took up my book. The bath steamed gently in front of the fire, vapours curled up like the genii from the bottle in Arabian Nights. The pictures on the wall seemed to sway and quiver in the ever-changing mists and dancing patterns of light and darkness in the room. I thought of the big red house on the far hillside, and wondered whether the inhabitants of the fourteen bathrooms were enjoying the sensation as much as I in my little round bath, but I longed to see a real bathroom with a fountain of water. In summer I had a daily tub of spring water in the attic, but I had to carry the water myself for this luxury.

Later, when I was acquainted with real bathrooms, I was

deeply disappointed. They had none of the beauty and glamour I had expected. They were hygienic cells with white walls and no furniture except a chair which looked forlorn and sad. Boiling water hissed cruelly as it spurted from a tap, and cold water had no sparkle or smell of woods and trees. There were no dancing shadows or firelight or carpets to step upon.

The exception was the bathroom of a friend in an old Cheshire house. In one corner of the pleasant room was the fireplace with bright fire and rugs before it. And at the opposite side stood the great mahogany bath. It was like a four-poster bed with golden-brown walls reaching to a canopy. The bath was raised on a polished platform and one walked up the step to enter, to turn the taps high in that wooden wall, and sink into the luxurious depths. Thick damask curtains hung round the sides, to screen the bather, and a lamp shone from the roof. The room had two doors, for it was the passageway to other bedrooms. The bather could sit in the warm bath behind those curtains and talk to the passers-by as they went from one room to another, or draw the sliding rings apart and gaze at the flickering fire across the way. So the ladies bathed in the eighteenth century, and so they bath now. The bathroom is unchanged, lavender-scented, bees-waxed, with windows looking out on the terraced garden and the marsh where white geese gather.

Visit to the Dentist

A visit to the dentist in my childhood was an event, almost a treat, for I had to beg permission from my father who had no money for dentists and thought it was a luxury when there was no toothache. We ate few sweets, and we seldom had toothache, but when we had a twinge the pain was eased by the application of vinegar and brown paper, warmed at the fire and bound on the cheek with a woollen bandage, and we lay down to sleep on the settle by the fire.

The druggist pulled out teeth at a shilling a tooth. Farm labourers went to him and returned with lurid tales of a great pincer thrust into their mouths and desperate struggles between the tooth and the strong arm of the druggist. Often they brought back the tooth for me to see the fangs.

Our infant teeth were helped out by a piece of cotton and a tug, but some children had the cotton fastened to a door which was suddenly shut and out came the tooth. It was a drastic act which was unpopular, and we never had this torture.

The solace for the loss of a tooth was the ritual that followed. The little tooth was sprinkled with salt, and put in the centre of a glowing fire, while we chanted the following incantation, as we stared at the flame of yellow:

> Old tooth, New tooth,
> Pray God send me a new tooth.

With this prayer our hopes were raised and we were content. As the tooth went on its journey we received a shining

126

new sixpence as a reward for bravery. It was a great occasion and we all firmly believed in the necessity of this burning of the tooth.

My little brother was taken by my mother to the first-class dentist in the small town some miles away. Mr. Fitzherbert belonged to a county family and he could be trusted.

The little boy sat in a chair and the dentist told him to open his mouth. At once he leapt up, as if sensing the danger, and ran round the surgery. My mother and the dentist chased him, but they could not catch him. He knocked over the furniture and fought and screamed, so my poor embarrassed mother apologized and took him out to the pony trap where my father was waiting. It was a shameful story, but the child was a hero. I was afraid I should not be welcomed after this affair, but I wanted to find out the mysteries of having a tooth stopped, and I had a small hole waiting. So I persuaded my father to give me the railway fare of fourpence return, and I said I would walk to the town over the hills to save the money. My mother made an appointment for a Saturday morning.

It was a great adventure to walk alone across the fields by the narrow green grassy track, and the Old Road, to go along a path which was mostly invisible, for it was used only by gypsies and beggars and the oatcake man, who knew this ancient secret way, which was a well-known path in my father's boyhood.

The main road was used by everybody, along the valleys by the side of the river, cutting the high rocks, winding through the villages, but it was too far for me, and my way wandered gently over the hills, in remote and flowery country. It was the track the ancient people walked or rode, when there was no lane, my father told me, and it

was easy to follow if I used my common sense. I believed
that the ancient Britons walked there, tribes who moved
across the ridges of the world. My way lay among fields
and woods, across country to avoid the roundabout road
which passed through the valleys. The train went through
some tunnels, but I went over the top, along the spine of
the hills. I started on an almost invisible footpath in the
fields, and I went through stiles and gates, each one
guarded by cattle or by lonely calves. Cows loved the

gates, they liked to see a stranger walking there, where
they congregated like countrymen viewing the scene. They
were always waiting, waiting, these dumb creatures whom
I longed to talk to, to be friends with, as I stroked their
heads and listened for a voice.

A thrush sang "Will ye do it? Will ye do it?" and the
cuckoo called "Cuckoo! Cuckoo!" All round was an unseen
vital life going on, eyes were watching me, butterflies

touched my arms, and spiders walked on my shoes. I had only to stand still and I was aware of the unseen, exciting world around me.

"Come on. Come on. Come on. Will ye do it?" said the thrush again and I obeyed and went on, avoiding the cow-pats, and hazards of the way, a grass snake slithering by the trough, a fox leaping a wall. I kept a lookout for a bull before I entered a field, and when I saw one I made a detour, keeping close to the wall and climbing over it when he was out of sight.

After passing through several fields, each with its guardian cattle, and picking foxgloves and wild roses on the way, I came to a pasture of rough grass, very steep, which was watered by a wild little stream, a baby stream, only a few inches wide in parts, but spreading out over marshy land. The ground was boggy and slippery and the water flowed several yards over the grass, where it sprang in little fountains from the earth. These springs were always pleasant, for many flowers grew on their verges.

Farm men put down a few stones for crossing the stream, but these had been disturbed by cattle, and each traveller had to make his own footbridge. I collected a few stones from the hillside and hopped across, standing for a minute in the centre to see the fountains and bubbles and to listen to the water.

Many birds gathered there, and flowers grew in the wet soil. Meadow sweet, forget-me-nots, primroses, ragged robin, a favourite of mine, some bluebells and marsh orchis, and clumps of delicate ferns. The path was completely lost in this network of springs of water.

At another place, close to the path there was a stone trough fed by a spring. Here I stopped to drink, cupping the clear water in my hand, as it sprang from a rock and fell in the trough. Every field had a spring which ran into a stone trough, moss-covered and half hidden in ferns, with a stone slab in front of it and a few rocks at the back to keep cattle from stepping directly in the water.

I found birds' nests and bees' nests, and the nests of ants, and at each I stopped and peered and wondered. There was a heap of stones, the relic of some ancient mining for lead, and there I hunted for fragments of Blue John spar, which I pocketed with glee. All this time I met nobody, and never in all my young life did I see a traveller on our old trackway.

I reached a wood of stunted dark trees, called "Kissing Wood", but who kissed there I did not know. It was sinister and dark, with very old and small gnarled trees, and the path through it was paved with irregular slabs of flat stone, for springs abounded and the way was rough and wet. Trees bent down to whip my face, trees caressed my cheeks with gentle touch, and some lashed at me. I might meet a gypsy there, or a vagabond, and I might be murdered and buried and forgotten for ever. A wolf might come out, a wolf which had been forgotten and hidden for a hundred years, and it would slay me. There were crackles and whispers and sighs, and no bird sang. I stepped softly on the stones, hurrying to get across this wet morass of little springs and devils and elves, all waiting for my body and soul.

I came out to a wild little pasture, where a fox climbed a limestone wall and a stoat ran out of the shadows. I was safe, I was free, for in the distance I spied the stile which led to a real road and humankind. I was like Christian in *Pilgrim's Progress*, I had passed through the terrors and Paradise lay before me. I slipped through the difficult stile, which was narrow and crooked and built on a stiff slope, as if to warn people not to venture through it, for it led to dangers unknown. I had passed through these perils and I entered a little hill village which always seemed to be forgotten. It was a straggling line of cottages, with here and there a tiny farm, and a shop. In one of the cottages lived our dressmaker, and I stared at the garden gate and the monkey-puzzle tree with a vision of the parlour and pins and tape-measure. Below the village street the ground dipped suddenly down to the river, a hundred feet below, for we were on the crest of the rocks, on the old road which was a high road three hundred years earlier, before the medieval bridge was built across the river. Horses and carts, charabancs and heavy drays went along the road deep in the valley, but the village road was almost deserted. The oatcake man lived there, and the mole-catcher, and the shepherd and the stone-mason who made stone ornaments.

I soon left the village and dived down through a gate, deep down, to the valley, to the town life I had avoided. A slender iron bridge, which was ugly, spanned the river, which was beautiful, and I walked on between the overhanging rocks to the town, to the houses with their trim gardens, and the paved footpaths. There the dentist had his surgery.

I was an hour late, as I rang the bell. I was hot and tired and my hands were filled with wild flowers, and my pocket was stiff with shells and bits of stone, with fossils and spar. I sat in the long cool waiting-room, which was indeed a waiting-room for me. I sat there for at least two hours until all the patients had gone, and it was my turn.

I did not mind, there were many magazines to read, and I never saw magazines at home. I read the *Strand* and the *Windsor*, I learned by heart a poem and memorized the music of the musical page in the *Strand*. I did the puzzles, and enjoyed every moment in that library of good things. Fairy-tale, detective tale, music and poetry, I absorbed them all before I was called to the back room.

The tall austere man was kind and gentle and silent. I enjoyed the whizzing buzzing drill when he murmured, "Tell me as soon as it hurts," and I liked the tilting chair, and the running water which stopped me from speaking. There was a trickling tap in the room which made a soft tune, five notes in succession, a musical air which I told him about when he finished. He had not noticed it, he told me, looking keenly at me. He told me to come again in a year and he shook my hand as if I were grown up.

It was a long wait for another visit, and I longed to read more magazines, and to know more about Louis de Rougement in the *Windsor*—or was it the *Strand*? I said good-bye and thanked him, and went in search of a shop where I could buy a penny bar of chocolate. I started off home, keeping the chocolate for the rigours of the Kissing Wood, sipping the water in the springs, stepping lightly over the marshy field, thinking of the stories I had read.

I climbed the hill to my home, thinking of all my adventures, but with the secrecy of a child I kept the best to myself, the stoat in Kissing Wood, the calves by a gate, the sound of the little dripping tap, the invisible something in the air, a flicker of light in the trees.

Now when I am going to the dentist, I must catch a diesel train to London, a noisy little train with no private carriages upholstered in velvet, a train which rushes through towns with rows of suburban houses, each with its neat garden, divided by narrow paths, and graced by one tree, probably an apple. I am much interested in these dolls'-house gardens, and the houses with their lines of washing, but the country has gone. I get a taxi at Marylebone and go to Wimpole Street, where some of the tall houses have blue plaques to remind us of the famous people who once lived there. I climb a flight of steps, and ring a bell. I am ushered into a waiting-room, a large room where solemn people sit in leather-lined chairs. Magazines are spread out on the centre polished table, but there is no journal with an exciting tale of adventure. I am punctual and I am sure I shall not have to wait more than a few minutes until I am called to enter the lift and ascend to the surgery.

I look round and wait with faint apprehension, for nobody looks happy or relaxed. Can it be that nobody likes a visit to the dentist? Suddenly my eyes are attracted to the great mantelpiece with its inlaid stones. This room was once the dining-room of a private household, wealthy people who had chosen to have a stone fireplace decorated with choice marble and spar. It must have been the pride of the head of the house, a hundred years ago. In the centre of the pattern is a translucent slice of polished Blue John, that lovely blue spar which was quarried in the hills of my youth and used for decorative vases and bowls and brooches.

I am suddenly transported to another time and place, I can smell the tossing river and the wet rocks and the limestone crags, and I can see the white rock with the Blue John treasured in many a cottage and hall, this same Blue John quarried from the mines, and fashioned by the men in cottages where they smoothed the stone and polished it by the aid of water running from the hills in little streams.

I look at the blue of violets in the stone on the mantelpiece, in London, and I see the land of my childhood, and I am going to the dentist, past a heap of stones with fragments from a mine, in a field. Nobody else is aware of this stone and the message. The door opens and a porter summons me to the room upstairs. I walk swiftly through, feeling elated, and looking forward to the tilting chair and the running water. The Scottish dentist comes to meet me. I mention the stone but he has never noticed it. I sit in the tilting chair, looking out on the tall faded brick house opposite, but I cannot read the words on the blue plaque. I am thinking of the haunted Kissing Wood, and the cuckoo, and the cows waiting at the gates. I hear the sound of running water, and I smell the wild flowers that lie on a chair near me. I am here, catching a vision of the immortality of another place, brought back by the inanimate, and given so freely to all who are waiting to receive these intimations.

The Prize

It was Prize Day at the village school. Mr. and Mrs. Garland were driving there to see Susan get her reward. They had been to the prize-giving before, when Susan was eight, and again when she was nine. They saw the procession of little boys and girls go up to the headmaster's desk, little boys with round red faces and necks squeezed in glazed collars, little girls with frizzed hair and sashes, but they waited in vain for Susan's name to be called. Margaret was sadly disappointed. She couldn't understand it at all. Susan, who was such a lively lass, good at her lessons, quick at sums, so neat a writer that she was entrusted to make out the milk tickets for the station-master to read; Susan who read from morning till night if she could get hold of a book; Susan whose Bible knowledge Margaret herself had superintended, never got a prize.

At last the farmer and his wife refused to go to the stifling schoolroom, to sit through a long December evening, away from their own fireside, in order to watch the children of other folk curtsy for books and their own child get nothing.

"Hold your peace! Say no more about it," said Tom, after the second fruitless journey. "I'm shut of it! All that way, taking the mare out at night, driving in the cold, just to listen to a lot of childer sing 'Men of Harlech' and 'Rule Britannia'. Not again."

"I think prizes are for attendances, Father," explained

Susan. "I don't attend enough to get a prize. If I'm late I lose my attendance."

"It's not your fault you are kept away," cried Margaret indignantly. "How can you be expected to go when the woods are deep in snow, and maybe you'd get lost in a snowdrift? You walk there in torrents of rain, and you come home with your umbrella blown inside out time and again. You get soaked to the skin, and you sit in your damp clothes all day. You ought to get a special prize for going at all in bad weather."

"The only thing I have against the school is that our Susan doesn't get a prize," said Tom Garland slowly. "It doesn't seem hardly fair that the little wench should walk all that way and come home by herself in the dark, and others, with only a step to go, should carry off those nice books. It doesn't seem hardly right to me."

"Some people's children have no distance at all to walk," added Margaret, exasperated with the injustice. "They start off when the bell has nearly finished ringing and they are in time, while Susan has to go through the wood with her dinner in her bag and sit in the cold play-ground to eat it, and come home with a lantern at night. They ought to give a prize for lessons, like they did when I was a child. Susan ought to get a special prize."

But the Government didn't give Susan a special prize, and Tom and Margaret wouldn't go to any more prize-givings.

It was true, some children lived only a short distance from the village school, and the schoolmaster's family went through a door from their living room into the classroom without even wetting the soles of their feet. Every one of them got a prize. It was doubtless a compensation for being the children of a schoolmaster and Susan was thankful to have escaped that blessing.

In summer it was easy to make attendances, and she ran through the woods with her skipping-rope in her hand and her sunbonnet hanging from her shoulders, but when November came there was a falling off that wrecked all hopes of a prize. She trudged along the road with her heart left at home by the warm fireside, she dragged her weary legs over the long lonely paths. The wind snarled like a wolf, it moaned and put cold paws on her neck. She drew her cloak more closely, but the wind tugged and tried to tear it away. Hat, cloak, dinner-bag, and umbrella, all dragged at Susan, and hindered her journey, making her late. There was the stick waiting for her and the loss of attendance. Then came winter's rain and snow, and days of illness. She came home wet to her chemise, her boots sodden with water so that Becky had to peel them off, her hair streaming and trickling in her neck, the umbrella blown away. She was undressed and wrapped in the old shepherd's plaid by the kitchen fire. She sat with eyes bright as flames and cheeks scarlet, while her clothes steamed on the iron rack and her stockings dried on the oven door.

Her wet cloak hung in the brewhouse all night against the warm wall, along with the men's coats and the sacks from their shoulders, and the water dripped to the stone floor and ran through a convenient square hole in the wall to the rocky hillside. In the morning the garments were dry as boards, and each one smelled of the sandstone benches and rabbit skins. Becky filled the brass bowl with warm water, and Margaret lifted the cold red feet and bathed them; she soaped them with yellow soap, and dried them on a soft towel, kneeling on the hearth before the shrouded figure like a Madonna before the Child. Warmed and dried, Susan ate her plate of Irish stew on the hearthstone by the blazing fire and a great content stole over her. It was splendid to be safe after the struggle against darkness and rain and lurking wolves and demons.

But sometimes Susan caught cold, and then she was dosed with linseed tea and liquorice, and her chest rubbed with strong-smelling oils. She was put to bed with a fire crackling in her bedroom. She drank the hot gruel with its dash of treacle, she sucked a cough lozenge, and she lay on the feather bed under the patchwork quilt. Cheerfully she bore her sore throat, as she listened to the wind blowing round the house, crying out to catch her. It was lovely to be ill, to have dainty morsels, to croak and cough and win attention and sympathy. Margaret read aloud to her, and recited the ballads of her own youth, and sang hymns to refresh her soul. It was all very pleasant, but with every day's absence from school the chance of a prize receded.

At last the little bearded man in a hard hat came to the house with his notebook and threats of a fine. The Government had sent him to see what had happened to

Susan Garland. Susan was hidden away as soon as the dog barked and Tom Garland spied the attendance officer coming up the hill. There was consternation at the farm, and fear of a county court summons.

Tom Garland spoke soothingly to him, of the frost damage and the sheep in lamb, and the political situation, but Margaret spoke up bravely of the difficulties of sending Susan to school in bad weather, and the risks of pumony. They offered him a glass of hot spiced elderberry wine, and hoped they were not bribing the Government. But they were always alarmed at his visit and Susan was packed off to school before she was really well.

It seemed to be as impossible for Susan to get enough attendances for a prize as for the Biblical camel to go through the eye of a needle. Susan had offered up prayers on Sundays at church, and by the bedside night and morning, as well as in many less conventional places, but her name was not read out as a prize-winner.

Although the chance of a prize was so remote nobody ever mentioned the subject, Susan brought home a fine certificate with a blue and gold border and her name written in large flowing characters:

"Award of Merit for an Essay on The Heart. Susan Garland."

The temperance reformer came to the village school and gave a talk on the entrancing subject of the Heart. Susan, like the other children, thought of the heart as a curved locket hung inside her breast, clean and dry like the silver heart she wore on Sundays. It ticked night and day, and never needed to be wound. It was the seat of the affections, the source of life, the treasure hidden in the casket of the body. If the heart stopped, death came. Some bold boys experimented, and held their breath till their faces were scarlet and their eyes bulged, but nobody could stop his heart from beating. In panics of fear, when a bull ran after Susan, and when the terrible evil ones stalked the woods, her heart beat madly, but it never betrayed her by stopping altogether. Susan had a sincere affection for her heart, and she was eager to know more about it.

Mrs. Garland dressed Susan in her best diaper pinafore and a clean print frock to go to the lecture on the Heart. It was a most important lecture, the first Susan had ever heard. All the boys and girls came to school that afternoon arrayed in special clothes, the boys with clean white collars, the girls in speckless pinafores. Their hands were scrubbed, their hair brushed, and they went to the big schoolroom where the lecturer stood talking to the headmaster.

The monitor put up the blackboard, and the head girl dusted a chair and brought a glass of water for the gentleman to drink. He wore a blue ribbon in his buttonhole, and the children whispered to one another. Some of them knew all about blue ribbons. Susan wanted to know too, but there was hardly time to tell. It was a ribbon badge you wore. You swore that you would never drink, and if you did you broke the pledge.

"What pledge?" asked Susan in an awed whisper.

"The blue ribbon pledge. So help me God. You couldn't wear the ribbon if you broke it. You'd be turned out of the Band of Hope."

"Eben Trout's father took the pledge after he'd been drinking, and he's never touched a drop since," whispered one little girl. "It kept him steady."

"My father belongs," said a boy proudly. "Does yours, Susan Garland?"

Susan shook her head. She was suddenly ashamed of her father and mother. They had no blue ribbons. Not only they had no blue ribbons, but Mrs. Garland had a glass of stout on Sundays. Becky fetched the bottle from the case in the calf-place. It came from their old friend the brewer. Worse than that, there was a bottle of rum in the Dark Passage. On cold winter nights when Tom Garland came home from work half frozen with the bitter wind, his eyes watering, his great body shivering as if with ague, the cure was a drop of rum in a saucer of scalding hot tea. It brought the red colour back to his cheeks, and removed the fatigue from his body. Susan liked the smell as it curled up in a fine vapour, and she liked the noise of the supping, and the return to health, for she was frightened when her father who was so strong was out on the hillside with the snow drifting and the wind blowing a hurricane from the north. Brown cream they called it, in joke.

But they had no blue ribbons. Even Susan couldn't wear one, for she had tasted strong drink and found it delicious. That was when the shooting-party lunches were held at the farm. The squire came with his house-party, gentlemen and ladies with guns, and the parlours were laid out for a splendid luncheon. The kitchen was invaded by an army of servants; footmen carried hampers of provisions, cooks brought copper saucepans shining like gold, and cheeses and bottles of wine. There were chickens, and turtle soup, and great sirloins of cold beef, skewered with silver. There was a deep rumble of voices and loud laughter when the parlour doors were open, and high feminine talk, very fine, when the footmen entered the second room where the ladies lunched. Ladies ran upstairs to the parlour bedroom and water closet, and men smoked in the hall. Outside in the cartshed a trestle table was set for the beaters, and others ate in the yard, sitting on the low walls and benches. A hundred people were served on the days when the farm was used for shooting parties. It was a great occasion, a day of pride.

Susan sat in the corner of the settle, hidden in the shadow, watching everything with wide eyes, but when the feast was over, and the voices were stilled, when the gentry walked out to the lawn to survey the bag of game laid out in symmetrical lines, and the beaters were starting off, and the servants were eating the remains of the food in

the kitchen, then Susan entered into her kingdom. She slipped quietly through the hall and pushed open the parlour door. The room was filled with blue smoke from cigars and the most entrancing smell pervaded everything. On the plates lay rinds of melon, grape skins and nutshells, peelings from golden apples and broken rolls of bread. Fruit was heaped on the sideboard on the green Wedgwood dishes that were Susan's great-grandmother's, but it wasn't Windystone fruit, and it would be taken away by the liveried servants. Wine-glasses were everywhere, the old cut glass from the cupboard, and in them were drops of ruby wine, and straw-coloured wine, and silvery wine. Susan went round the room tasting from each glass, putting it gently to her lips, and tilting it up. The touch of the slender-stemmed glasses, the diamond flash of their facets as she twirled them in the sun, the tinkle of them as she put two together, enchanted her. She drained every glass in the room with enjoyment, so that she felt one of the party. Then she strolled away to see the pheasants and rabbits, none the worse for her experience.

Susan couldn't truthfully say she was teetotal, for she liked the taste of that mixture of wines, drunk from the beautiful glasses, and she looked forward to the next shooting party.

The headmaster called for silence, and the lecturer began. He unfolded a picture of the human body, with a red heart, not at all like Susan's heart, washed whiter than snow, but similar to a bullock's heart. Susan didn't believe her body was like that, and she was glad when the picture was rolled up. The lecturer talked in a pleasant manner, and made the children feel at ease. Their hearts, he said, were like houses, and there were four rooms inside, auricles and ventricles. That was exciting indeed, and they all imagined the little curved house inside their breasts with four tiny rooms, two upstairs and two down. He drew it on the blackboard, a most satisfactory heart. He explained how it beat, and they counted their own heart-beats as he spoke. But alcohol was bad for it; it turned the heart to stone!

He fumbled in a bag and brought out a bottle with a frog pickled in alcohol. That was what would happen to the human heart. He brought out other strange and repulsive

143

things in bottles—snakes, and grey objects. The little girls shivered, but the boys laughed boldly.

Finally he offered certificates for the best essays on the heart, and he asked children to go home and tell their parents what he had said, and to ask if they could join the Band of Hope.

Susan hurried home in great trepidation.

"Mother! You mustn't drink stout any more. Nobody must drink anything except water and tea," she cried, shaking Margaret's arm in her anxiety. "Mother, if you do your heart will be turned to stone."

Margaret laughed till the tears came, but Susan choked back angry sobs. It was unfair to make fun.

"Mother, it will! It will! I've seen it! I've seen things turned to stone by alcohol. You'll die if your heart is stone. It will stop beating and you'll be dead."

Susan spoke passionately, striving to move her mother, angered that her protests were ignored. The lecturer had said so. He had shown a stone frog. Margaret's heart would be petrified like the birds' nests in the petrifying wells if she ever drank another glass of stout.

But Margaret continued to have her Sunday treat, and Tom had his saucer of tea with a spot of rum, and nothing happened to their hearts. They would never get blue ribbons to wear. Susan sat in the schoolroom and wrote a careful essay on "The Heart". Her reward was the fine certificate.

It was a great occasion at Windystone, and the certificate was handed from one to another to admire. Susan hoped her mother would have it framed, but Margaret shook her head. It would be like boasting to put a framed certificate on the wall. It was enough to have gained it and Susan must be content to peep at it as it lay in the bureau along with less showy and more valuable certificates for piano playing.

One winter's day Susan's name was read out as a prize-winner. Susan went very white, her heart struggled in her breast as if it would fly away like a bird. Her prayer had been answered. So all things were possible to God, who took care of her in the perils of the wood. Now He had helped her to get a prize. Susan was convinced she had not done it by herself. Only God could have managed to get those attendances up to the right number.

The farm brimmed over with happiness. The trees sang, and the fields clapped their hands. The chairs and tables rejoiced with Susan, and the grandfather clock ticked more loudly than ever. It wasn't often a school prize had come to Windystone. Maybe it was the first time, for they didn't have prizes when Tom Garland went to school. Birch rod and the strap, and never a reward at all.

Margaret spread the good news in the distant villages.

"Why, of course. Susan isn't a gaubie," said her friends, the farmers' wives, the squire's housekeeper, and Susan's god-mother, Miss Dickory. None of them had children and they didn't know the strict laws which governed school boards.

"But they don't give prizes for headpieces," said Margaret. "It's for the number of attendances. Don't you think it is unfair? They ought to give a special prize to Susan, as I've said for years. I expect it will be a beautiful book. Well, she's got one at last, and we are driving to the school for prize-giving to see her get it."

Some little girls went to school on the morning of prize-day with their hair done up in a dozen little plaits which stuck out like the quills of a porcupine. Others had curling rags like white buttons round their heads. Even the schoolmistress wore her fringe in curling-pins, hidden under a velvet toque. Susan would gladly have submitted to plaits but Mrs. Garland wouldn't hear of it. If Nature had intended Susan to have curly hair she would have been born with curls.

There were no lessons. Instead they practised singing "The Men of Harlech" and "The Minstrel Boy", which they gave every year. Then they walked out and made their bows and curtsies to an imaginary prize-giver, and back they went to their homes.

Margaret had washed and ironed the white China silk dress the night before, and it lay ready spread over a chair. Susan could hardly wait for the afternoon to pass, but the farm work had to be done and the prize-giving was not till evening. She put on clean black stockings with neat darns at the knees, and clean white drawers and cotton petticoat. She slipped the China silk dress over her head, and Becky helped to fasten the yoke, and arrange the full skirt.

"Nay, missis! You'd best do it. My fingers is more used to suckling calves than catching plaguey buttons like these," groaned Becky as the tiny pearl buttons slipped their moorings and came undone as fast as she put them through their loops. Mrs. Garland tied the old salmon silk sash that Susan had worn for years round her daughter's waist, and arranged the broad folds in concertina pleats. She took the real tortoiseshell comb from the tea-urn, where it lay coiled round the infuser. In its teeth she stuck a little bow of salmon-pink ribbon, like a tropical butterfly, for Susan's dark hair. It was the first time such a luxury had been seen at the farm, but the lady's maid at the Court had told Mrs. Garland that it was the latest fashion for young ladies in London.

The Prize

Margaret hoped Susan would not be filled with vanity, but there was no looking-glass for the girl to view herself in any comfort. Susan said she felt thirsty, and she took a mug to drink from the trough. The manœuvre was guileful, for the clear surface of the water made an admirable mirror, and she leaned over the deep drinking-trough and stared at herself and the butterfly bow for a whole minute before she dipped the mug and broke the water into a thousand intersecting waves. She watched the glittering vibrating ripples with their fragments of reflections, windy sky and bare damson trees, and she swirled the water in greater waves, upon which the salmon-pink bow flickered and swung above her small, pointed, ever-changing face.

"Good gracious, Susan! Will you never have sense? A great girl going to get a prize, playing with the water!" Margaret was indignant, and Susan rose abashed from her watery encounter. She had forgotten everything in the lure of the shadowy girl who looked back at her from the water's depths.

Nathaniel was polishing the trap lamps, and getting the best harness ready, but they couldn't start till the milking was done. Seven o'clock was the time of the concert that preceded the prize-giving, when all the parents would have returned from work in mill and farm and field, changed their clothes, and had a bite of food.

Susan was eager to be off, but Tom watched the grandfather clock and took out his own big turnip watch and held it up, comparing them. They listened at the door for the train in the valley. It was no use to be there before anyone else, and Susan must eat a good tea so that she could curtsy nicely to the Honourable Miss who was giving away the prizes.

Susan knew how to do it, for she had curtsied all the way home through the woods, swaying to the beech trees, bending low to the hazels. Not too deep, and not a bob, but a slow bending of one knee, and a recovery without overbalancing.

At last it was time to start, and they climbed into the trap, seated close to one another for warmth, wrapped round with rugs and cloaks. The nosebag with a feed of hay for the mare was pushed under the seat, with her own yellow rug. The side-lamps were lighted, and the beams made cones of gold on the low walls and the rocky ground. Tom Garland chirruped gently and spoke in warm intimate tones to the mare, and she pricked her ears, hearkening to his beloved voice. The wheels ground noisily on the stones, and the vehicle bounced and swayed down the hill, lurching drunkenly when a large stone got in its way, swinging to right and to left with three people swaying in unison, and three odd shadows flickering on the gorse bushes and brambles. The mare couldn't go through the wood, along the break-neck path Susan took each day. It had to make a great curve down the hill and along the turnpike, moving in an arc encompassing the beech trees.

They reached the hamlet, where little groups of dusky people were walking towards the school. Susan looked down at them with pity and pride, hoping they would recognize her behind the fast-trotting little mare, driving in state to get her prize. The trap lamps flashed on upturned faces, and one and another hailed them.

Everything was different on that night of nights. The woods were full of magic, the sky was alive with watching, whispering, singing stars. There were voices in the air, and flashes from the cottages in the darkness of the hillsides. They drove past the cottage where dwelt the young woman whose baby had no father. They stopped for the mare to drink at the trough where the frog once lived which went down a boy's throat with a gulp of water and hatched a family of frogs inside him. There was the mill dam where anyone might be drowned dead, and anyone would be damned who didn't call it "dom".

The road was lined with pitfalls, which only Susan could see, but their power for evil was lost when she sat safe between her parents on the high seat of the bouncing, rolling, little pony-trap, with the strong, harsh smell of the mare, and the odour of the leather reins, the fragrance of her father's hair-oil, and her mother's handkerchief and seal-skin muff. Susan wouldn't have changed places with the Queen of England herself.

They put up the pony at Sawyer's Farm, down by the mill-stream, and they walked to the school in the darkness. The long narrow schoolroom was crowded with parents and children, fathers with hair pomaded and plastered on their foreheads, little boys in starched white turned-down collars and bows, girls in their Sunday clothes, and their hair crimped like angels, mothers in hats of many fashions. They all sat in the long narrow desks, wedged close together, the butcher, the baker, the miller, the postmaster, the head gardener, just as if they were going to have lessons, but there was a buzz of conversation that would never have been allowed in school hours. Susan was amazed at the boldness of those who dared speak aloud when the headmaster was in the room.

She glanced hastily at the desk for the cane, but it wasn't in its usual place. It had been tactfully removed, and Susan was thankful, for only that week she had felt its stinging bite upon the palms of her hands and she had nursed the swollen fingers, wrapped in her pinafore. All the hamlets round were chattering like a wood of magpies and the cane wasn't there!

Tom Garland walked into the room with slow dignity, and looked round with calm stare. He knew he could never get his huge frame into the narrow school seats. He stood like a good-tempered giant, his square hat in his hand, his large bewhiskered face smiling at the folk, nodding to one and another acquaintance, who called "Evening, Mester Garland", and he replied, "Good evening, John", or Matthew or Nathaniel, calling each one by his Christian name, for they were much younger than he, and he had known them as boys.

Mrs. Garland waited behind him, gently smiling at every child, her face radiant with happiness and pride. The schoolmaster himself came up and shook their hands and called with imperious gesture to a boy to bring them chairs.

He tinkled his bell, and there was silence. Everybody obeyed him at once with no hesitation. He beckoned and the children rose and sang a hymn. Then came the concert with "Men of Harlech" sung by the boys, "Blue Bells of Scotland" sung by the girls, "The Minstrel Boy" sung by the lowest classes, and "Rule Britannia" shouted by everybody.

They represented England, Ireland, Scotland, and Wales, said the schoolmaster, and they all clapped for the four divisions of their country, although nobody knew anything of those far regions Scotland, Ireland, and Wales, except the Scottish head gardener.

The schoolmaster played a few bars of each song on his fiddle and then beat time with his bow, swooping and diving with hands outstretched and shoulders bowing in the manner of a great conductor. He spoke of Beethoven and Handel with friendly ease, and urged the parents to give their children more music. He snapped his fingers, and beckoned to four little boys, his pupils, who sawed away at their little red fiddles, their faces scarlet with emotion, their hands sticky with sweat and fright, while four others held on to the music, which slithered and slipped from the music stands. He shook his open palms at them, begging them to play softly, and nodded to them, asking them to accelerate. It was all very noble, and the audience thumped the desks till the inkwells rattled, and stamped the floor till a thick dust arose. The shrill squeak of the violins made Susan leap in her chair; she was proud of the boys and proud of her schoolmaster. If only her parents would allow her to learn the fiddle instead of the piano! But it was a boy's instrument, and not for girls.

Somebody recited "Half a league! Half a league! Half a league onward", in a magnificent manner. Amanda Baker, Emily's sister, followed with "Curfew shall not ring to-night". Speeches were made by the vicar of the hamlets and the minister, and all praised the headmaster for his work.

The pupil teachers in their velvet dresses, with lace collarettes round their necks and ringlets falling on their shoulders, sat like seraphs. Children shuffled and coughed and sweated, and left the room urgently; they eased their tight collars, which cut their necks in red weals, they scratched their heads. The room got stifling, and the parents moved uneasily in their cramped seats. The lamps hanging from the ceiling sent out dark smoke and long points of flame, and the monitors were summoned to stand on desks and lower the wicks. Proudly they did their duty, and heavily they leapt down. This attention to the lamps made a friendly feeling in the room, and brought the speeches down from the high levels to which they had flown. Not everyone could understand the language of the vicar's friend, who had been talking politics, but all knew about smoky lamps, and the way they should be treated. Beyond the lamps' circle the room was in shadowy darkness, and the cases of fossils and specimens glittered like evil eyes behind their glass doors. Paper pictures of "The Sower Sowing his Seed" and "The Prodigal Son" swung on their rollers, caught by a draught from the high window, but no air came to the packed people on their narrow forms.

Susan's eyes were on the pile of books by the master's desk. One of those books was for her, and she stared at the red and blue covers as if she could turn the invisible pages and read the enchanting tales within. One of those books! There was no method of knowing which was the prize. It was an important moment of life, a stile from one field to another. She had started school at seven and now she was eleven, going on twelve. Would it be Shakespeare's plays with *A Midsummer Night's Dream*, that fairy story she wanted to read? Or would it be poetry, Longfellow, or Tennyson? Or a tale like *Ben Hur*?

Characters from all the books she knew moved through her mind in a series of bright pictures—King Arthur and Lancelot, Robinson Crusoe and Man Friday, Topsy and Eva, Maggie Tulliver and Tom, Mr. Pickwick, Barnaby Rudge and all the rich company of Dickens. They laughed and beckoned and curtsied as they sprang out of the books lying on the deal table, and the girl sat with a wistful smile on her face, watching their movements, listening to their talk, half rising as they nodded to her and waved their hands.

But everyone began to clap, and the Honourable Miss stood up with the first book for the schoolmaster's Amanda. The procession to the desk began. Children walked out as their names were called. Little boys forgot to bow, or bowed too late, or lugged a lock of hair, grabbed the prize, and lurched back with sheepish grins, in a great hurry to get to the seats. Little girls simpered and curtsied and bobbed. Susan sat trembling with elation, filled with desire for the beautiful unknown, with pages unopened, and magical tales of fairy and dwarf, tales to enchant the winter months and bring roses from the snowy skies.

Mrs. Garland placed a warm hand upon hers in sympathy, but Susan dragged herself quickly away. She couldn't bear any sympathy. The pile of books had dwindled, when Susan's name was called. She had only just scraped the minimum attendances, and she was near the end. All the beautiful books had gone, the reds and golds were already in the chubby grimy hands of other children, but a dull cover often holds a wonderful tale, as Susan knew very well. Robinson Crusoe himself had a dark maroon coat under his brown paper wrapping.

The clapping rose louder than ever, swelled by the mighty palms of Tom Garland, who clapped his hands as if he were scaring crows from the cornland, or summoning a harvester from a distant field. It was a roar of a clap, thunderous. Margaret, who sat starry-eyed, with tears not far away, clapped with all her might, and Susan stepped from her seat and sidled past the legs of the boys.

"Susan Garland has a long way to come to school," said the schoolmaster, bending towards the Honourable Miss, who looked astonished at so much applause. "She well deserves her prize."

Susan curtsied neatly and took the book with whispered thanks and a shy glance of gratitude to the furred and scented lady. Then she walked slowly back to her place, oblivious of the stamping feet. She held the prize close to her heart, pressed tight in her arms, not daring to look at the title.

"What have you got, Susan Garland?" cried Emily Baker, with a grown-up smile of patronage, and she stretched out her arm imperiously. Emily had left school, and she was going to a training college.

Susan held out the book obediently, ignoring her mother who was embarrassingly happy, talking to children around her, and behaving in the most indecorous manner. Mothers ought not to speak at prize-givings.

"Oh, that! I'm sorry for you! *The Old Helmet*. It's a religious book," scoffed Emily maliciously, and she pushed the book away. "You won't like it. It's awful!"

"Yes, I shall. I've always wanted it," whispered Susan quickly. She had never heard of the title, but a helmet was iron, and with it went a sword and a suit of armour, and a knight to wear them. It must be a good book with such a title.

Mrs. Garland took the cheap little book and turned the badly printed pages. It wasn't much to look at, certainly, and she had expected a book in leather binding with gilt edges for her Susan, but it was a good religious book, and that was everything. She saw the passages from the Scriptures, and holy words sprinkling the pages.

Susan saw them too with a sinking of her heart. The Old Helmet was the helmet of righteousness, and not the helmet of a crusader. But it didn't matter, it was her prize, and she had won it. Her father and mother were delighted, but Susan sat very still, unheeding the chatter. Nobody should ever know she minded about the book. Her heart had been set on magic and wonder, on a tale exquisite as gossamer, a Midsummer Night's Dream of a tale, and she had received a stone, an old helmet in answer to her prayers.

The Prize

She sat in the trap, squeezed between her father and mother as they drove home down the long valley to the riverside. In the sky were a million stars winking at her, and the bare trees reached up their branches and caught them like fish in dark nets, but they always escaped. Then down sped a star, falling into the illimitable, and Susan made a little wish. She knew something. Oh! She knew something! It was air, going on for ever! No, not air, ether, filling the space outside the world, and heaven was toppled out of the sky and the golden throne was somewhere else. She had heard the schoolmaster talking to the pupil teachers about it. It was a secret not to be told. She sang a wordless song of ecstasy about it, and held up her face to the icy breath of that magical ether. In the west a planet shone and Margaret cried out in wonder.

"That's a new star, Tom. I've never seen that one before," she said to her husband. "It wasn't there before, I'm sure."

Perhaps a new star was born that night, no planet age-old. But Tom shook the reins and chirruped to the mare.

"I've seen it afore, many a time," said he. "It's always been somewhere or other."

In the air was the sweet sharp smell of snow, an exciting smell which sent the little mare galloping madly down the white road, shying at the moon-shadows, and made Susan's spirit leap to the moon above. She was riding her own white chariot and a lunar rainbow hung round her like a scarf, dripping its colours on the shifting clouds. Susan nodded her head to the moon, her old companion, the one who never deserted her for long, who came back with a regularity which was printed in Tom's pocket-book. Susan looked at the moon, and the moon looked serenely back at Susan. Her tranquillity filled the girl's

155

heart to bursting. They knew each other, those two. They had always known.

Susan leaned back between her parents, and kept her eyes on the glimmering face in the sky, to catch the swift motion of that heavenly body. The book, clasped in her arms, was forgotten. The tales she wanted were all about her, in the enchanted woods, high in the moon mountains, and deep in the earth.

The First Day

The autumn term had already begun when Susan started off to her new school. With a fine cloth satchel strapped on her back like a boy, instead of the little blue linen bag in her hand, Susan got ready. In the satchel were her sandwiches for dinner and a bun for tea, with a bottle of milk and an apple. It would be eleven hours before she returned.

She was dressed soberly and stiffly, in new boots and her plain dress, but there was an air of gaiety in the tartan tam-o'-shanter Margaret had made to match the lining of the cloak. Susan cocked it on her dark hair with a pheasant feather in the side. The cloak pleased her, for Louisa had made it well, and it swung from her shoulders like wings, and flew behind her held by its crossed straps when she ran. When the rains and snows of winter came she could wrap it completely round her body and defy any storm.

The milk cart with its load of churns was ready in the yard when Susan finished breakfast and said good-bye and "God bless you". Half-past seven and no time to lose. She sat on the slippery seat, sliding forward over the mare's back as the cart rattled and jolted down the steep hill. Margaret stood on the bank waving to her. Dan led the mare and opened the gates, propping them until his return. Susan turned round at the corner where the lane twisted under the wood, and waved to her parents.

There was no bunch of flowers for the teacher, no skipping rope, and no old men and women to greet her at their doorways, but there was a sense of great adventure, a

journey, new companions, a new world. The milk churns
banged together and Susan jolted with them, three bright
churns with brass labels and one girl. They rolled over
stones, and tilted on the curved banks, for Dan drove
recklessly, springing on the step and leaping down, and
then standing like a charioteer, and lashing with the reins.
He was too turbulent a fellow to have a whip, but he cut a
switch from the hedge and hurried the mare forward. It
was a breakneck, exhilarating ride, and Susan's cheeks
burned with the spitting rain and the beating wind.

She felt happy as a king to be a real traveller, one of the
little company on the platform. She listened to the talk of
the agent for linseed cake, who supplied the farm, and the
young porter. They stood in the little room where the
lamps were trimmed, and argued about county cricket.
The farm lads ran their trolley across the line for the up

train, and everybody waited for the express to rush through. Then the milk train came rumbling into the station, and the agent for cow cake and the porter and the bank clerk all came out. Susan saw three or four schoolgirls leaning from a window to see the new girl, but they made no sign to her and she was too shy to join them.

It was a slow journey, but far too quick for Susan, who was suddenly shy and fearful of reaching the end. At each station there was a load of milk churns, with attendant farm lads pushing and pulling at the trolleys, and shouting as they hauled the churns aboard, or held up the train while a galloping horse dashed up and churns were seized by willing hands and rolled along the platform. Every farm in the countryside sent its milk away, and in every station yard the horses stood with bent heads tied to posts, waiting for the empty churns to be thrown out of the vans and loaded ready for home. Susan regarded them with great interest, for a farm was known by its turn-out, by the shining brass labels, or by the unpolished dirty churns. Many a milk cart showed the poverty of the farm, and many a farmer drove his own cart, and hauled his churns to the train along with the young lads.

The guard, with his buttonhole of geraniums, cheered her heart, for she remembered him on her scholarship journey. He walked up and down the train with a fine air of possession, carrying his green flag, beckoning to a late comer to hurry, stopping the train for a tardy passenger, and helping the solitary first-class gentleman to his first-class carriage. The engine driver leaned out at each station and gossiped with friends, and the porters nodded and talked. One of them was the brother of a grammar schoolgirl, and the girls leaned out to speak to him. The passengers were always the same, farmers and drovers on market days, a little group of dressmaker's apprentices, a couple of bank clerks, and one first class who kept the train waiting for a minute or two and was treated with great deference by guard and porter and engine driver alike. A few boys and girls joined the train on the way, the girls demure, giggling softly and glancing with lowered eyes at the boys, who pushed and swaggered and larked, scattering their books on the platform, careless as puppies.

Susan sat close to the window, staring out with interest, hearing names bandied, admiring a fair-haired girl who hung from the train, beckoning her friends to enter, shaking her flaxen mop like a flag, and peering at Susan with slant eyes. Susan smiled back from her corner, and the girl laughed and turned to speak to others in the carriage.

She followed the children down the hill to the school, past the banks of heavy golden gorse, which flowers as long as kissing is in season, past the lovely shallow river, moving so slowly, and past the ivy-covered inn. She was proud to be going to school in such an enchanting place, with a great church above the houses, and the Duke's woods behind her. . . .

The bevy of girls kept close to their fair-haired friend, and Susan wished she too had a flaxen mane to blow out in the stinging rain. Her cloak swept back and she was proud of it, and proud of the schoolbag and its bright buckles, and the testimonial which lay within. They would receive her as one of their own quite soon.

When she went into the school all her self-confidence fell away and she was assailed by shyness. She was overcome with deep humility when she went up the flight of stone stairs with a crowd of staring town girls who eyed her coldly, disdainfully, who walked with arms encircling each other, and called each other Diana, Claire, Virginia, Letitia, and flaunted little gold and enamel watches pinned on their round bosoms, and silver bracelets on their arms, and curls and ringlets on their heads. Susan felt like a wren in her plain brown dress, with never an ornament, not even the silver brooch. In the crowded little cloakroom it was worse, for there wasn't a peg for her cloak, and she hadn't brought any slippers, or soap, or a cookery apron or a science apron. "No talking," said the mistress, and she sailed out of the room like a ship in deep water, with a train sweeping the floor after her. Bells rang, and everyone hurried out, masters in mortar boards, gloomy and black-gowned, big boys and girls, everyone looked grown-up. There was a babel of voices, and a curious odour, not of humanity as in the village school, but of something extraordinary, a smell which came almost visibly down the passage, penetrating the cloakroom and hall.

Girls shuddered delicately and turned up their little noses, and made wry faces of elegant disgust, as they told each other "Sulphuretted hydrogen".

Sulphuretted hydrogen! Susan was enchanted with the new word, and she forgot her embarrassment and shyness in utter bliss that she was breathing air tinged, nay saturated, with such romantic odours. That was what she longed to meet, a genie from the science room. But as she stood, absorbing the chemistry room smells, staring down the passage at the closed door of the paradise where the alchemist lived with his retorts and crucibles, his crystals and poisons, she was pounced on by a master. "The scholarship girl? Susan Garland? You go downstairs to the head-master's room. He wants to see you. Knock on the door and wait outside till he tells you to go in. Get along with you! Get! Quick!"

Susan tapped at the door and waited, but nobody came. Papers rustled inside, and children murmured in the next room. . . . At last the door was flung open and the headmaster came tearing out, nearly knocking her over. Susan looked up at him with earnest eyes, a supplicant.

"Who's this? The scholarship girl? Why didn't you knock? What's your name? You're a train-girl, aren't you! Your father's a farmer!"

He looked contemptuously at her, withering her with his unconcealed irritation, and pushed her out of the doorway. His cold hard voice hurt her, his contempt seared her. A scholarship girl! A train-girl! She realized with a flash of amazement that instead of an honour it was a disgrace to have a scholarship, and it was an added stigma to travel by train. She lived at a farm, and the schoolmaster was a Londoner. He was made of a different material, fine and rich, and she was of the soil. It was a topsy-turvy world, but Susan was grateful that a Londoner should be there. She was humble before one who had heard the bells of Bow and seen the River Thames.

She went to a classroom and a bright little mistress gave her a desk all to herself. It was a home, that yellow-stained desk, with a brass inkwell lid and a space for books and a ridge for her feet to rest lifted from the dust of the floor. She felt at peace after the discord, she was on an island, and the touch of the wood was comforting, and the darkness of the desk's interior a refuge from eyes staring. She put her pencil box within and stayed a moment hidden, drawing strength and reserves to help her. Then she shut the lid and faced the room. The round-faced young mistress was smiling, and her nice white teeth had a gap big enough for a sixpence to slip through. That was a sign of fortune, Becky had told Susan. She wore a brooch in the shape of a gold wish-bone. She must be a person favoured by the unseen ones, those who bring luck.

"Susan Garland? Have you done any French? Or Algebra? Or Euclid?"

The blissful day had begun and Susan cared nothing for scholarship or snobbery as she listened to lessons and shared somebody's books. At break she went into the school garden where the grass was not to be walked upon. Girls came up and spoke to her, friendly girls, who questioned her, and took her to the cookery room for the next lesson.

Suddenly a thick-set girl detached herself from a group and shot an odd question at Susan.

"Have you a bathroom in your house?" she asked in a loud voice which carried across the room. She smiled a little sidelong smile and looked to see if the others were listening. "Have you a bathroom? You're a train-girl, aren't you? You're a scholarship girl?"

Susan confessed they had no bathroom. Heads nodded, skirts flounced, and the dark girl turned away.

"She says she lives in a house without a bathroom."

It was a damning fact, no bathroom could ever be built at Windystone, or the troughs might dry up. All the springs on the hillside would be dislocated, and the cattle would have nothing in their troughs. Drinking water for cattle and horses and man came before bathrooms. Susan was disconcerted. She hoped they wouldn't pursue the question of bathrooms. Now if this Eva had asked if there was a water closet, Susan could have boasted that there was and the seat was made from a church pew and the tassel was thick red velvet. As for the view from the window, it was superb. But other girls had no bathrooms and there was an embarrassed air as they looked at one another. Even as they stood undecided the cookery mistress came across and interrupted.

"When will you be returning to Manchester, Eva?" she asked quietly. "You are only here for this term, are you not? I expect you find our ways different from yours. Many of us in the country have no bathrooms, but we have other consolations."

Eva blushed and retreated among the girls, but Miss Dobbin's grey eyes twinkled. She was a friendly woman, with no awe-inspiring cap and gown, but a white apron and starched cuffs. She asked Susan where she lived and smiled when she heard. She knew the villages round Windystone and she too came by train.

Susan lifted a grateful heart for this merciful deliverance from the town-bred Eva. She was thankful for the homely comfortable appearance of the teacher, who was already busy with a pasteboard, a rolling-pin, and a yellow bowl. Her thoughts flashed to the farm, to a white apron hanging behind a door, to an immense rolling-pin like a truncheon, and an ancient pastry board which had been in the dairy for fifty years. They were so human they had voices which spoke to her, and here were similar utensils, small and neat, ready for the lesson. Gossip was checked, the bathroom question faded away, and the teacher made Yorkshire pudding and rock buns and soup from little red seeds called lentils which Jacob used for his mess of pottage.

. . . Eva was heavy-fingered, and the mistress rebuked her so that she sulked and scowled, but the others chatted gaily and there was the friendly feeling of a kitchen as the girls weighed and mixed and beat up eggs. They cooked in a bright oven with a grand fire blazing up the chimney, and they scrubbed the boards with hot water which came from taps in the wall. It was a cheerful lesson, in which Susan was at home, for the cookery room had taken on the likeness of the kitchen at Windystone, and the girls tasted their cakes and chatted to the mistress in a familiar way which was unlike a school.

Then came books, many books to fill the yellow desk, books with bright covers and ravishing smells, books that Susan got for nothing at all. Blue for Latin, red for *Rémi et ses amis*, green for algebra, and dirty brown for Euclid. That was the best book of all, very old and ragged, with long-legged triangles striding about and circles revolving dizzily, and squares where Susan could sit in a corner and strange stiff language which old Euclid himself might have spoken. Susan thought it was ancient magic. The axioms were the wisdom of Solomon, the postulates were poetry. The propositions were worth knowing. They made up for the difficulty of French, which was pronounced quite differently from the way it was spelt.

Susan drifted from one classroom to another, following the girls and boys to rooms of queer ugliness and wizardry. White heads perched on window-sills, and a hand hung here and a foot dangled there. Ghostly and disembodied they were, like a horrible wax-work show. She took an intense dislike to the plaster casts, and their stony eyes gazing sightless from the high ledges. Everything was bare, and she was filled with nostalgia for the fossils and specimens of rock, the jugs of wild flowers, and the ripening tomatoes which had decorated the village schoolroom. There was no playground. When Susan followed the line of children to the chemistry room she was dazzled by the wonders. The energy of the school was concentrated in that strong-smelling room. Gas jets burned with invisible flames upon the benches, crystals blue and green lay imprisoned in jars, a glass retort bubbled, as if an alchemist had a brew within, tripods strode the benches, and exquisite porcelain crucibles, fit for a goblin's cookery lesson, simmered with molten globules inside. Over all hovered the smell of sulphuretted hydrogen from the stink cupboard. "Rotten eggs" they called it.

What matter that the master flung himself down the room with black gown sweeping, the corners burnt, the front stained with acid, to box a boy's ears, and hurl bitter words at the girls. He was the wizard who knew the secrets, the source of light and sound, the ways of the sun and stars, the meaning of waves and shadows. He made no distinction between the town girl and the train-girl, and the scholarship girls were scolded equally with the daughters of the vicar.

All he cared for was his work, and quickly the children realized it and made allowances for his anger. Susan leaned forward, her gaze concentrated on experiments, then she went to her bench and set up the apparatus. She forgot everything else, all the discomforts and difficulties, in her eager desire to find out, to seek for the hidden substance.

So the day moved on, the sun trundled slowly up its great cart-road in the sky, the longest day Susan had ever known. Surely the sun crawled like a snail up that invisible highway, rutted and sown with unseen stars? It was a lifetime, that day. Susan was born, she grew old, and died while the minutes ticked away. Those hours were packed with strange and disconcerting and wonderful experiences, with bliss and misery, with the memory of the harsh tones of the head-master, and the warm kindness of others. Cold and fire intermingled, bitter and sweet, peace and war.

The First Day

At five o'clock she walked up the station hill and joined the other girls on the platform. The cookery mistress sat there, in her grey coat and skirt, and she was reading a novel by Trollope. She talked to the girls and asked them to sit down by her, and showed them the book. She told Susan that in summer there would be a sewing class and she would read aloud just as Susan's mother read to her.

The train came in and Susan rode with the other girls in their carriage. They opened their bags and took out cakes and bread and jam, and Susan hungrily ate the cake which tasted of home. Home! She had forgotten it except for the brief moment in the cookery room. She had forgotten all about Windystone, and her father and the horses and Becky. She had been on another planet, out of her country world, away on a strange star.

The train roared through the tunnels, it puffed and wheezed with a great hiss of steam as it stopped at stations, it clanked with armour in the sidings, and all was very still. Then off it rumbled again, and the metals sang, and the steel bands that stretched along the river and road flashed white. Telegraph wires rose and fell in gentle rhythm, and the distant hills moved graciously across the sky. That was something to ask about, why the blue hills sailed like ships and the near hedgerows ran like racehorses.

But Susan crouched on the seat, and did her algebra, sharing somebody's bottle of ink, comparing answers, listening to the lessons which were going on all round.

She called good-bye as girls alighted at the different stations; she knew them all, even the white-maned Lily. There was the good sounding clatter of churns and the shouts of the farm boys, and the smell of the country, and happiness, everybody going home to a good meal and company round the fire. They passed the stud-farm where one scholarship girl lived, and the mill by the stream where another lived, and they waved from the window to mothers who were watching the train.

Then Susan herself got out, and said good-bye to the three remaining ones, Mary, the daughter of the Scottish head-gardener, Alice, the daughter of a housekeeper, and Lily, the well-dressed fair one, who might have been the child of a duke, but her father kept a draper's shop.

The milk cart was at the station, and Susan rode along by the river, and away up the hill, silent, tired, and strangely happy. She rolled about among the empty churns, hungry for food.

"Did you like it?" asked Margaret, pressing the girl's cold cheeks with eager lips and sweeping back her hair. "Was it nice? Did you like the lessons?"

She drew the cloak from Susan's shoulders, and removed her hat, and stroked back her hair with a hungry longing, wishful to share every experience of her growing daughter, knowing it was impossible to see into that heart.

"Yes," said Susan. "It was lovely. I've got lots of books, Euclid and algebra, and chemistry, and I learned how to make lentil soup."

"And the head-master? Was he pleased to see you?"

"Oh yes," said Susan, quietly.

"I'm sure he was." Margaret nodded her head with satisfaction, and turned to the oven for the plate of mushrooms. "You've got a scholarship, and he must have been very glad to see you."

Susan gasped, and then held her peace.

"I want a white apron for cookery, and a black apron for chemistry, and a tunic for gymnastics, and a hat badge, Mother. And after Christmas there's a dancing class. Can I learn dancing, Mother? It costs seven-and-sixpence. Do let me, after Christmas.''

"I don't know, child. Seven-and-six is a lot of money, and you want these other things. But we'll see. I'll see what I can save by then.''

Susan hastened through the meal and ran out to the fields. Only there could she calm her excited spirits. She would go once again through all the experiences and trials of the day, and tell them to her beloved trees and stone walls and horses. She would relate her story to all those who would listen, the invisible ones who lived out there.

She climbed up the fields in the dusk, to the highest point by the top gate, and there she sat, looking down at the farm on its ledge of rock, at the hills in the distance, and the misty river half hidden in the valley. She reconstructed the events of the day, she poured out her heart, not speaking aloud, but communing as animals talk, and the wind and the sky all heard. She was a little scholarship girl at school, in the market town, where the London teacher lived, but here, on the hill-top, she was queen of her kingdom.

They all knew her, and she was part of them. The trees were her foster mothers, the fields her companions and the stone walls a great company of rough old friends, the best of all. Under her feet she felt the grass, her own land, welcoming her, caressing her. Above her was the sky, God's roof to her little world. She stayed there, watching the evening mists rise in the valley. The farm lay in the blue upper vapours of its little plateau, but down in the curved valley a moving cloud of whiteness hid the road and river. The sea was encroaching, the tide was coming up to make the farm an island, and she was a mariner going home. The birds of evening sang, and a star came out in the western sky, and another joined it. The trees stood darkling against the violet hills, and the green colour of night spread over the west. Then a light shone from the kitchen window, the beacon for which she had been waiting. Home called her, in a clear high voice, thin and cold and infinitely pure, a voice which seemed to come out of the sky. She could no longer restrain herself. It was the house calling and calling her, drawing her back to it, and if she didn't answer she might be shut out for ever.

She sprang to her feet and raced down the grand slopes, and she felt she had grown wings which were lifting her from the earth so that she scarcely touched the ground in her flight. Her eyes were fixed on that golden eye which was like a lighthouse to the ship out on the stormy wave.

The gate of home shone white in the dim light, and shadows lay under the yews. Smoke curled among the high elm boughs from two chimneys and there was a warm comforting look about the house. Duchess whinnied at the gate, nosing the latch, and Susan grabbed her forelock and led her to the stable. The calves mooed mournfully and the dog leapt to welcome her.

Susan ran through the wicket gate, to the back door. She lifted the iron latch very softly, and peered inside the kitchen, as if she were a stranger. Margaret stood by the table, dressed in her old cream holland dress, starched and crackling, with the little round gold brooch at her neck. There was a smell of roast apples and bread, and new milk from the cans on the floor. Tom Garland sat by the fire reading the newspaper, and the servant boy was unlacing his boots and hunting under the frilled cover for his slippers.

She pushed open the door, and laughed as she entered. It was home, and she had heard its voice.